FIRST ENCOUNTER

FIRST ENCOUNTER

By

JOHN DOS PASSOS

PHILOSOPHICAL LIBRARY

New York

TO THOSE
WITH WHOM I SAW ROCKETS IN
THE SKY A CERTAIN EVENING AT
SUNSET ON THE ROAD FROM ERIZE-
LA-PETITE   TO   ERIZE-LA-GRANDE.

A PREFACE TWENTY-FIVE YEARS LATER

It just happens that I'm looking over this little book with a view to its publication at a time when I'm in the middle of writing up the notes of another tour to another front in another war. This narrative was written more than a quarter of a century ago by a bookish young man of twenty-two who had emerged half-baked from Harvard College and was continuing his education driving an ambulance behind the front in France. The young man who wrote it was about the same age as so many of the young men I was seeing and talking to last winter in the Pacific. All the time I was trying to imagine how I'd be thinking and feeling if I were that young man again, really in the war up to my ears, instead of being a middle-aged literary man getting a couple of quick looks at it as a correspondent.

There would be a number of differences.

For one thing I think the brutalities of war and oppression came as less of a shock to people who grew up in the thirties than they did to Americans of my generation, raised as we were during the quiet afterglow of the nineteenth century, among comfortably situated people who were confident that industrial progress meant an improved civilization, more of the good things of life all around, more freedom, a more humane and peaceful society. To us, the European war of 1914-1918 seemed a horrible monstrosity, something outside of the normal order of things like an epidemic of yellow fever in some place where yellow fever had never been heard of before.

The boys who are fighting these present wars got their first ideas of the world during the depression years. From the time they first read the newspapers they drank in the brutalities of European politics with their breakfast coffee.

War and oppression in the early years of this century appeared to us like stinking slums in a city that was otherwise beautiful and good to live in, blemishes that skill and courage would remove. To the young men of today these things are inherent deformities of mankind. If you have your club foot you learn to live with your club foot. That doesn't mean they like the dust and the mud and the fatigue and the agony of war or the oppression of man by man any better than we did. But the ideas of these things are more familiar.

Looking back it is frightening to remember that naive ignorance of men and their behavior through history which enabled us to believe that a revolution which would throw the rascals out of the saddle would automatically, by some divine order of historical necessity, put in their places a band of benign philosophers. It was only later that some of us came to understand that when you threw out King Log you were like as not to get King Stork in his place.

Nobody had given a thought to educating us in the traditional processes of self-government or in the rule that individual liberty, wherever it has existed in the world, has come as the result of a balance between the rights and duties of various contending individuals or groups, every man standing up for himself within the framework of a body of laws and customs. Having no knowledge of the society we had grown up in, or of the traditional attitudes that had produced in us the very ethical bent which made war and tyranny abhorrent to us, we easily fell prey to the notion that by a series of revolutions like the Russian the working people of the world could invent out of their own heads a reign of peace and justice. It was an illusion like the quaint illusion the early Christians had that the world would come to an end in the Year One Thousand.

In reporting a conversation we had with a congenial bunch of Frenchmen one night in a little town where the division was en repos, I tried to get some of this down on paper. As an American unaccustomed to the carefully articulated systems of thought which in those days were still part of the heritage of the European mind, I remember being amazed and delighted to meet men who could formulate their moral attitudes, Catholic, Anarchist, Communist, so elegantly. Reading it over I find the chapter scrappy and unsatisfactory, but I am letting it stand because it still expresses, in the language of the time, some of the enthusiasms and some of the hopes of young men already marked for slaughter in that year of enthusiasms and hopes beyond other years, the year of the October Revolution.

It was this sanguine feeling that the future was a blank page to write on, focusing first about the speeches of Woodrow Wilson and then about the figure of Lenin, that made the end of the last war so different from the period we are now entering. Perhaps the disillusionments of the last quarter of a century have taught us that there are no short cuts to a decent ordering of human affairs, that the *climb back up out of the pit of savagery to a society of even approximate justice and freedom must necessarily be hard and slow. We can only manage one small step at a time. The quality of the means we use will always determine the ends we reach.* ·

Last winter, talking to the young men out in the Pacific I found that most of them just hoped that what they would return to after the war would not be worse than what they had left. This is not an age of illusions. We can only hope that it will become an age of clear thinking.

JOHN DOS PASSOS

Providence, Massachusetts. April 26, 1945.

CHAPTER I

IN the huge shed of the wharf, piled with crates and baggage, broken by gangplanks leading up to ships on either side, a band plays a tinselly Hawaiian tune; people are dancing in and out among the piles of trunks and boxes. There is a scattering of khaki uniforms, and many young men stand in groups laughing and talking in voices pitched shrill with excitement. In the brown light of the wharf, full of rows of yellow crates and barrels and sacks, full of racket of cranes, among which winds in and out the trivial lilt of the Hawaiian tune, there is a flutter of gay dresses and coloured hats of women, and white handkerchiefs.

The booming reverberation of the ship's whistle drowns all other sound.

After it the noise of farewells rises shrill. White handkerchiefs are agitated in the brown light of the shed. Ropes crack in pulleys as the gang planks are raised.

Again, at the pierhead, white handkerchiefs

and cheering and a flutter of coloured dresses. On the wharf building a flag spreads exultingly against the azure afternoon sky.

Rosy yellow and drab purple, the buildings of New York slide together into a pyramid above brown smudges of smoke standing out in the water, linked to the land by the dark curves of the bridges.

In the fresh harbour wind comes now and then a salt-wafting breath off the sea.

Martin Howe stands in the stern that trembles with the vibrating push of the screw. A boy standing beside him turns and asks in a tremulous voice, "This your first time across?"

"Yes. .... Yours?"

"Yes. . . . I never used to think that at nineteen I'd be crossing the Atlantic to go to a war in France." The boy caught himself up suddenly and blushed. Then swallowing a lump in his throat he said, "It ought to be time to eat."

> *"God help Kaiser Bill!*
> *O-o-o old Uncle Sam.*
> *He's got the cavalry,*
> *He's got the infantry,*
> *He's got the artillery;*
> *And than by God we'll all go to Germany.*
> *God help Kaiser Bill!"*

The iron covers are clamped on the smoking-room windows, for no lights must show. So the air is dense with tobacco smoke and the reek of beer and champagne. In one corner they are playing poker with their coats off. All the chairs are full of sprawling young men who stamp their feet to the time, and bang their fists down so that the bottles dance on the tables.

"God help Kaiser Bill."

Sky and sea are opal grey. Martin is stretched on the deck in the bow of the boat with an unopened book beside him. He has never been so happy in his life. The future is nothing to him, the past is nothing to him. All his life is effaced in the grey languor of the sea, in the soft surge of the water about the ship's bow as she ploughs through the long swell, eastward. The tepid moisture of the Gulf Stream makes his clothes feel damp and his hair stick together into curls that straggle over his forehead. There are porpoises about, lazily tumbling in the swell, and flying-fish skim from one grey wave to another, and the bow rises and falls gently in rhythm with the surging sing-song of the broken water.

Martin has been asleep. As through infinite mists of greyness he looks back on the sharp hatreds and wringing desires of his life. Now a leaf seems to have been turned and a new white page spread before him, clean and unwritten on. At last things have come to pass.

And very faintly, like music heard across the water in the evening, blurred into strange harmonies, his old watchwords echo a little in his mind, Like the red flame of the sunset setting fire to opal sea and sky, the old exaltation, the old flame that would consume to ashes all the lies in the world, the trumpet-blast under which the walls of Jericho would fall down, stirs and broods in the womb of his grey lassitude. The bow rises and falls gently in rhythm with the surging sing-song of the broken water, as the steamer ploughs through the long swell of the Gulf Stream, eastward.

"See that guy, the feller with the straw hat; he lost five hundred dollars at craps last night."

"Some stakes."

It is almost dark. Sea and sky are glowing claret colour, darkened to a cold bluish- green to westward. In a corner of the deck a number of men are crowded in a circle, while one shakes the dice in his hand with a nervous quiver that ends in a snap of the fingers as the white dice roll on the deck.

"Seven up."

From the smoking-room comes a sound of singing and glasses banged on tables:

"Oh, we're bound for the Hamburg show,
To see the elephant and the wild kangaroo,
An' we'll all stick together
In fair or foul weather,
For we're going to see the damn show through!"

On the settee a sallow young man is shaking the ice in a whisky-and-soda into a nervous tinkle as he talks:

"There's nothing they can do against this new gas. ... It just corrodes the lungs as if they were rotten in a dead body. In the hospitals they just stand the poor devils up against a wall and let them die. They say their skin turns green and that it takes from five to seven days to die — five to seven days of slow choking."

"Oh, but I think it's so splendid of you" — she bared all her teeth, white and regular as those in a dentist's show-case, in a smile as she spoke—"to come over this way to help France."

"Perhaps it's only curiosity," muttered Martin.

"Oh no. ... You're too modest. ... What I mean is that it's so splendid to have understood the issue. . . . That's how I feel. I just told dad I'd have to come and do my bit, as the English say."

"What are you going to do?"

"Something in Paris. I don't know just what, but I'll certainly make myself useful somehow." She beamed at him provocatively. "Oh, if only I was a man, I'd have shouldered my gun the first day; indeed I would."

"But the issues were hardly ... defined then," ventured Martin.

"They didn't need to be. I hate those brutes. I've always hated the Germans, their language, their country, everything about them. And now that they've done such frightful things..."

"I wonder if it's all true..."

"True! Oh, of course it's all true; and lots more that it hasn't been possible to print, that people have been ashamed to tell."

"They've gone pretty far," said Martin, laughing.

"If there are any left alive after the war they ought to be chloroformed.... And really

I don't think it's patriotic or humane to take the atrocities so lightly.... But really, you must excuse me if you think me rude; I do get so excited and wrought up when I think of those frightful things ... I get quite beside myself; I'm sure you do too, in your heart. ... Any red-blooded person would."

"Only I doubt ..."

"But you're just playing into their hands if you do that. ... Oh, dear, I'm quite beside myself, just thinking of it." She raised a small gloved hand to her pink cheek in a gesture of horror, and settled herself comfortably in her deck chair. 'Really, I oughtn't to talk about it. I lose all self-control when I do. I hate them so it makes me quite ill. ... The curs! The Huns! Let me tell you just one story. ...... I know it'll make your blood boil. It's absolutely authentic, too. I heard it before I left New York from a girl who's really the best friend I have on earth. She got it from a friend of hers who had it directly from a little Belgian girl, poor little thing, who was in the convent at the time.... Oh, I don't see why they ever take any prisoners; I'd kill them all like mad dogs."

"What's the story?"

"Oh, I can't tell it. It upsets me too much.

... No, that's silly, I've got to begin facing
realities. ... It was just when the Germans
were taking Bruges, the Uhlans broke into
this convent. ... But I think it was in Lou-
vain, not Bruges. . . . I have a wretched me-
mory for names. ... Well, they broke in, and
took all those poor defenceless little girls...."

"There's the dinner-bell."

"Oh, so it is. I much run and dress. I'll have
to tell you later. ..."

Through half-closed eyes, Martin watched
the fluttering dress and the backs of the neat
little white shoes go jauntily down the deck.

The smoking-room again. Clink of glasses
and chatter of confident voices. Two men
talking over their glasses.

"They tell me that Paris is some city."

"The most immoral place in the world,
before the war. Why, there are houses there
where . . ." his voice sank into a whisper.
The other man burst into loud guffaws.

"But the war's put an end to all that. They
tell me that French people are regenerated,
positively regenerated."

"They say the lack of food's something
awful, that you can't get a square meal. They
even eat horse."

"Did you hear what those fellows were saying about that new gas? Sounds frightful, don't it? I don't care a thing about bullets, but that kind o' gives me cold feet. ... I don't give a damn about bullets, but that gas. ..."

"That's why so many shoot their friends when they're gassed. ..."

"Say, you two, how about a hand of poker?"

A champagne cork pops.

"Jiminy, don't spill it all over me."

"Where we goin', boys?"

"Oh, we're going to the Hamburg show
To see the elephant and the wild kangaroo,
And we'll all stick together
In fair or foul weather,
For we're going to see the damn show through!"

CHAPTER II

BEFORE going to bed Martin had seen the lighthouses winking at the mouth of the Gironde, and had filled his lungs with the new, indefinably scented wind coming off the land. The sound of screaming whistles of tug-boats awoke him. Feet were tramping on the deck above his head. The shrill whine of a crane sounded in his ears and the throaty cry of men lifting something in unison.

Through his port-hole in the yet colourless dawn he saw the reddish water of a river with black-hulled sailing-boats on it and a few lanky little steamers of a pattern he had never seen before. Again he breathed deep of the new indefinable smell off the land.

Once on deck in the cold air, he saw through the faint light a row of houses beyond the low wharf buildings, grey mellow houses of four storeys with tiled roofs and intricate ironwork balconies, with balconies in which the ironwork had been carefully twisted by artisan long ago dead into gracefully modulated curves and spirals.

Some in uniform, some not, the ambulance men marched to the station, through the grey streets of Bordeaux. Once a woman opened a window and crying, "Vive l'Amérique," threw out a bunch of roses and daisies. As they were rounding a corner, a man with a frock-coat on ran up and put his own hat on the head of one of the American who had none. In front of the station, waiting for the train, they sat at at the little tables of cafés, lolling comfortably in the early morning sunlight, and drank beer and cognac.

Small railway carriages into which they were crowded so that their knees were pressed tight together—and outside, slipping by, blue-green fields, and poplars stalking out of the morning mist, and long drifts of poppies. Scarlet poppies, and cornflowers, and white daisies, and the red-tile roofs and white walls of cottages, all against a background of glaucous green fields and hedges. Tours, Poitiers, Orleans. In the names of the stations rose old wars, until the flood of scarlet poppies seemed the blood of fighting men slaughtered through all time. At last in the gloaming, Paris, and, in crossing a bridge over the Seine, a glimpse of the two linked towers of Notre-Dame, rosy grey in the grey mist up the river.

"Say, these women here get my goat."

"How do you mean?"

"Well, I was at the Olympia with Johnson and that crowd. They just pester the life out of you there. I'd heard that Paris was immoral, but nothing like this."

"It's the war."

"But the Jane I went with ..."

"Gee, these Frenchwomen are immoral. They say the war does it."

"Can't be that. Nothing is more purifying than sacrifice."

"A feller has to be mighty careful, they say."

"Looks like every woman you saw walking on the street was a whore. They certainly are good-lookers though."

"King and his gang are all being sent back to the States."

"I'll be darned! They sure have been drunk ever since they got off the steamer."

"Raised hell in Maxim's last night. They tried to clean up the place and the police came. They were all soused to the gills and tried to make everybody there sing 'The Star Spangled Banner'."

"Damn fool business."

Martin Howe sat at a table on the sidewalk under the brown awning of a restaurant. Opposite in the last topaz-clear rays of the sun, the foliage of the Jardin du Luxembourg shone bright green above deep alleys of bluish shadow. From the pavements in front of the mauve-coloured houses rose little kiosks with advertisements in bright orange and vermilion and blue. In the middle of the triangle formed by the streets and the garden was a round pool of jade water. Martin leaned back in his chair looking dreamily out through half-closed eyes, breathing deep now and then of the musty scent of Paris, that mingled with the melting freshness of the wild strawberries on the plate before him.

As he stared in front of him two figures crossed his field of vision. A woman swathed in black crepe veils was helping a soldier to a seat at the next table. He found himself staring in a face, a face that still had some of the chubbines of boyhood. Between the palebrown frightened eyes, where the nose should have been, was a triangular black patch that ended in some mechanical contrivance with shiny little black metal rods that took the place of the jaw. He could not take his eyes from the soldier's eyes, that were like those of a hurt animal, full of meek dismay. Someone plucked at Martin's arm, and he turned suddenly, fearfully.

A bent old woman was offering him flowers with a jerky curtsy.

"Just a rose, for good luck?"

"No, thank you."

"It will bring you happiness."

He took a couple of the reddest of the roses.

"Do you understand the language of flowers?"

"No."

"I shall teach you. ... Thank you so much. ... Thank you so much."

She added a few large daisies to the red roses in his hand.

"These will bring you love. ... But another time I shall teach you the language of flowers, the language of love."

She curtseyed again, and began making her way jerkily down the sidewalk, jingling his silver in her hand.

He stuck the roses and daisies in the belt of his uniform and sat with the green flame of Chartreuse in a little glass before him, staring into the gardens, where the foliage was becoming blue and lavender with evening, and the shadows darkened to grey-purple and black. Now and then he glanced furtively, with shame, at the man at the next table. When the restaurant closed he wandered through the unlighted streets towards the river listening to the laughs and conversations that bubbled like the sparkle in Burgundy through the purple summer night.

But wherever he looked in the comradely faces of young men, in the beckoning eyes of women, he saw the brown hurt eyes of the soldier, and the triangular black patch where the nose should have been.

CHAPTER III

AT Epernay the station was wrecked; the corrugated tin of the roof hung in strips over the crumbled brick walls.

"They say the Boches came over last night. They killed a lot of permissionaires."

"That river's the Marne."

"Gosh, is it? Let me get to the winder."

The third-class car, joggling along on a flat wheel, was full of the smell of sweat and sour wine. Outside, yellow-green and blue-green, crossed by long processions of poplars, aflame with vermilion and carmine of poppies, the countryside slipped by. At a station where the train stopped on a siding, they could hear a faint hollow sound in the distance: guns.

Croix de Guerre had been given out that day at the automobile park at Chalons. There was an unusually big dinner at the wooden tables in the narrow portable barracks, and during the last course the General passed through and drank a glass of champagne to the health of all present. Everybody had on his best uniform and sweated hugely in the narrow, airless building, from the wine and the champagne and the thick stew, thickly seasoned, that made the diner's main course.

"We are all one large family," said the General from the end of the barracks. . . "to France."

That night the wail of a siren woke Martin suddenly and made him sit up in his bunk trembling, wondering where he was. Like the shriek of a woman in a nightmare, the wail of the siren rose and rose and then dropped in pitch and faded throbbingly out.

"Don't flash a light there. It's Boche planes."

Outside the night was cold, with a little light from a waned moon.

"See the shrapnel!" someone cried.

"The Boche has a Mercedes motor," said someone else. "You can tell by the sound of it."

"They say one of their planes chased an ambulance ten miles along a straight road the other day, trying to get it with a machine-gun. The man who was driving got away, but he had shell-shock afterwards."

"Did he really?"

"Oh, I'm going to turn in. God, these French nights are cold!"

The rain pattered hard with unfaltering determination on the roof of the little arbour. Martin lolled over the rough board table, resting his chin on his clasped hands, looking through the tinkling bead curtains of the rain towards the other end of the weed-grown garden, where, under a canvas shelter, the cooks were moving about in front of two black steaming cauldrons. Through the fresh scent of rain-beaten leaves came a greasy smell of soup. He was thinking of the jolly wedding-parties that must have drunk and danced in this garden before the war, of the lovers who must have sat in that very arbour, pressing sunburned cheek against sunburned cheek, twining hands callous with work in the fields.

A man broke suddenly into the arbour behind Martin and stood flicking the water off his uniform with his cap. His sand-coloured hair was wet and was plastered in little spike to his broad forehead, a forehead that was the entablature of a determined rock-hewn face.

"Hello," said Martin, twisting his head to

look at the newcomer. "You section twenty-four?"

"Yes. . . . Ever read 'Alice in Wonder-land'? " asked the wet man, sitting down abruptly at the table.

"Yes, indeed."

"Doesn't this remind you of it?"

"What?"

"This war business. Why, I keep thinking I'm going to meet the rabbit who put butter in his watch round every corner."

"It was the best butter."

"That's the hell of it."

"When's your section leaving here?" asked Martin, picking up the conversation after a pause during which they'd both stared out into the rain. They could hear almost constantly the grinding roar of camions on the road behind the café and the slither of their wheels through the mud-puddles where the road turned into the village.

"How the devil should I know?"

"Somebody had dope this morning that we'd leave here for Soissons to-morrow." Martin's words tailed off into a convictionless mumble.

"It surely is different than you'd pictured it, isn't it, now?"

FIRST ENCOUNTER

They sat looking at each other while the big drops from the leaky roof smacked on the table or splashed cold in their faces.

"What do you think of all this, anyway?" said the wet man suddenly, lowering his voice stealthily.

"I don't know. I never did expect it to be what we were taught to believe. . . . Things aren't."

"But you can't have guessed that it was like this . . . like Alice in Wonderland, like an ill-intentioned Drury Lane pantomime, like all the dusty futility of Barnum and Bailey's Circus."

"No, I thought it would be hair-raising," said Martin.

"Think, man, think of all the oceans of lies through all the ages that must have been necessary to make this possible! Think of this new particular vintage of lies that has been so industriously pumped out of the press and the pulpit. Doesn't it stagger you?"

Martin nodded.

"Why, lies are like a sticky juice over-spreading the world, a living, growing fly-paper to catch and gum the wings of every human soul . . . And the little helpless buzzings of honest, liberal, kindly people, aren't they like the thin little noise flies make when they're caught? "

"I agree with you that the little thin noise is very silly," said Martin.

Martin slammed down the hood of the car and stood upright. A cold stream of rain ran down the sleeves of his slicker and dripped from his greasy hands.

Infantry tramped by, the rain spattering with a cold glitter on grey helmets, on gun-barrels, on the straps of equipment. Red sweating faces, drooping under the hard rims of helmets, turned to the ground with the struggle with the weight of equipment; rows and patches of faces were the only warmth in the desolation of putty-coloured mud and bowed mud-coloured bodies and dripping mud-coloured sky. In the cold colourlessness they were delicate and feeble as the faces of children, rosy and soft under the splattering of mud and the shagginess of unshaven beards.

Martin rubbed the back of his hand against his face. His skin was like that, too, soft as the petals of flowers, soft and warm amid all this dead mud, amid all this hard mudcovered steel.

FIRST ENCOUNTER

He leant against the side of the car, his ears
full of the heavy shuffle, of the jingle of
equipment, of the splashing in puddles of
water-soaked boots, and watched the endless
rosy patches of faces moving by, the faces
that drooped towards the dripping boots that
rose and fell, churning into froth the soupy,
putty-coloured mud of the road.

The schoolmaster's garden was full of late
roses and marigolds, all parched and bleached
by the thick layer of dust that was over them.
Next to the vine-covered trellis that cut the
garden off from the road stood a green table
and a few cane chairs. The schoolmaster,
something charmingly eighteenth-century
about the cut of his breeches and the calves
of his legs in their thick woollen golf-stock-
ings, led the way, a brown pitcher of wine
in his hand. Martin Howe and the black-
haired, brown-faced boy from New Orleans
who was his car-mate followed him. Then
came a little grey woman in a pink knitted
shawl, carrying a tray with glasses.

"In the Verdunois our wine is not very
good," said the schoolmaster, bowing them
into chairs. "It is thin and cold like the cli-
mate. To your health, gentlemen."

"To France."

"To America."

"And down with the Boches."

In the pale yellow light that came from among the dark clouds that passed over the sky, the wine had the chilly gleam of yellow diamonds.

"Ah, you should have seen that road in 1916," said the schoolmaster, drawing a hand over his watery blue eyes. "That, you know, is the Voie Sacrée, the sacred way that saved Verdun. All day, all day, a double line of camions went up, full of ammunition and ravitaillement and men."

"Oh, the poor boys, we saw so many go up," came the voice, dry as the rustling of the wind in the vine-leaves, of the grey old woman who stood leaning against the schoolmaster's chair, looking out through a gap in the trellis at the rutted road so thick with dust, "and never have we seen one of them come back."

"It was for France."

"But this was a nice village before the war. From Verdun to Bar-le-Duc, the Courrier des Postes used to tell us, there was no such village, so clean and with such fine orchards." The old woman leaned over the schoolmaster's shoulder, joining eagerly in the conversation.

[33]

"Even now the fruit is very fine," said Martin.

"But you soldiers, you steal it all," said the old woman, throwing out her arms. "You leave us nothing, nothing."

"We don't begrudge it," said the schoolmaster, "all we have is our country's."

"We shall starve then. . . ."

As she spoke the glasses on the table shook. With a roar of heavy wheels and a grind of gears a camion went by.

"Oh good God!" The old woman looked out on to the road with terror in her face, blinking her eyes in the thick dust.

Roaring with heavy wheels, grinding with gears, throbbing with motors, camion after camion went by, slowly, stridently. The men packed into the camions had broken through the canvas covers and leaned out, waving their arms and shouting.

"Oh, the poor children," said the old woman, wringing her hands, her voice lost in the roar and the shouting.

"They should not destroy property that way," said the schoolmaster. . . . "Last year it was dreadful. There were mutinies."

Martin sat, his chair tilted back, his hands trembling, staring with compressed lips at the men who jolted by on the strident, throbbing camions. A word formed in his mind: tumbrels.

In some trucks the men were drunk and singing, waving their bidons in the air, shouting at people along the road, crying out all sorts of things: "Get to the front!" "Into the trenches with them!" "Down with the war!" In others they sat quiet, faces corpselike with dust. Through the gap in the trellis Martin stared at them, noting intelligent faces, beautiful faces, faces brutally gay, miserable faces like those of sobbing drunkards.

At last the convoy passed and the dust settled again on the rutted road.

"Oh, the poor children!" said the old woman. "They know they are going to death."

They tried to hide their agitation. The schoolmaster poured out more wine.

"Yes," said Martin, "there are fine orchards on the hills round here."

"You should be here when the plums are ripe," said the schoolmaster.

A tall bearded man, covered with dust to the eyelashes, in the uniform of a commandant, stepped into the garden.

"My dear friends!" He shook hands with

the schoolmaster and the old woman and saluted the two Americans. "I could not pass without stopping a moment. We are going up to an attack. We have the honour to take the lead."

"You will have a glass of wine, won't you?"

"With great pleasure."

"Julie, fetch a bottle, you know which. . . . How is the morale?

"Perfect."

"I thought they looked a little discontented."

"No. . . . It's always like that. . . . They were yelling at some gendarmes. If they strung up a couple it would serve them right, dirty beasts."

"You soldiers are all one against the gendarmes."

"Yes. We fight the enemy but we hate the gendarmes." The commandant rubbed his hands, drank his wine and laughed.

"Hah! There's the next convoy. I must go."

"Good luck."

The commandant shrugged his shoulders, clicked his heels together at the garden gate, saluted, smiling, and was gone.

Again the village street was full of the grinding roar and throb of camions, full of a frenzy of wheels and drunken shouting.

"Give us a drink, you."

"We're the train de luxe, we are."

"Down with the war!"

And the old grey woman wrung her hands and said:

"Oh, the poor children, they know they are going to death!"

CHAPTER IV

MARTIN, rolled up in his bedroll on the floor of the empty hayloft, woke with a start.

"Say, Howe!" Tom Randolph, who lay next him, was pressing his hand. "I think I heard a shell go over."

As he spoke there came a shrill, loudening whine, and an explosion that shook the barn. A little dirt fell down on Martin's face.

"Say, fellers, that was damn near," came a voice from the floor of the barn.

"We'd better go over to the quarry."

"Oh, hell, I was sound asleep!"

A vicious shriek overhead and a shaking snort of explosion.

"Gee, that was in the house behind us...."

"I smell gas."

"Ye damn fool, it's carbide."

"One of the Frenchmen said it was gas."

"All right, fellers, put on your masks."

Outside there was a sickly rough smell in the air that mingled strangely with the perfume of the cool night, musical with the gurgling of the stream through the little valley where their barn was. They crouched in a quarry by the roadside, a strangling, half-naked group, and watched the flashes in the sky northward, where artillery along the line kept up a continuous hammering drumbeat. Over their heads shells shrieked at two-minutes intervals, to explode with a rattling ripping sound in the village on the other side of the valley.

"Damn foolishness," muttered Tom Randolph in his rich Southern voice. "Why don't those damn gunners go to sleep and let us go to sleep? . . . They must be tired like we are."

A shell burst in a house on the crest of the hill opposite, so that they saw the flash against the starry night sky. In the silence that followed, the moaning shriek of a man came faintly across the valley.

Martin sat on the steps of the dugout, looking up the shattered shaft of a tree, from the top of which a few ribbons of bark fluttered against the mauve evening sky. In the quiet he could hear the voice of men chatting in the dark below him, and a sound of someone whistling as he worked. Now and then, like some ungainly bird, a high calibre shell trundled through the air overhead; after its noise had completely died away would come the thud of the explosion. It was like battle-dore and shuttlecock, these huge masses whirling through the evening far above his head, now from one side, now from the other. It gave him somehow a cosy feeling of safety, as if he were under some sort of a bridge over which freight-cars were shunted madly to and fro.

The doctor in charge of the post came up and sat beside Martin. He was a small brown man with slim black moustaches that curved like the horns of a long-horn steer. He stood on tip-toe on the top step and peered about in every dirction with an air of ownership, then sat down again and began talking briskly.

"We are exactly four hundred and five mètres from the Boche. . . . Five hundred mètres from here they are drinking beer and saying, 'Hoch der Kaiser.' "

"About as much as we're saying 'Vive la République,' I should say."

"Who knows? But it is quiet here, isn't it? It's quieter here than in Paris."

"The sky is very beautiful to-night."

"They say they're shelling the Etat-Major to-day. Damned emubusqués; it'll do them good to get a bit of their own medicine."

Martin did not answer. He was crossing in his mind the four hundred and five mètres to the first Boche listening-post. Next beyond the abris was the latrine from which a puff of wind brought now and then a nauseous stench. Then there was the tin roof, crumpled as if by a hand, that had been a cook shack. That was just behind the second line trenches that zig-zagged in and out of great abscesses of wet, upturned clay along the crest of a little hill. The other day he had been there, and had clambered up the oily clay where the boyau had caved, in, and from the level of the ground had looked for an anxious minute or two at the tangle of trenches and pitted gangrened soil in the direction of the German outposts. And all along these random gashes in the mucky clay were men, feet and legs huge from clotting after clotting of clay, men with greyish-green faces scarred by lines of strain and fear and boredom as the hillside was scarred out of all semblance by the trenches and the shell-holes.

"We are well off here," said the doctor again. "I have not had a serious case all day."

"Up in the front line there's a place where they've planted rhubarb. . . . You know, where the hillside is beginning to get rocky."

"It was the Boche who did that. . . .We took that slope from them two months ago. . . . How does it grow?"

"They say the gas makes the leaves shrivel," said Martin, laughing.

He looked long at the little ranks of clouds that had begun to fill the sky, like ruffles on a woman's dress. Might not it really be, he kept asking himself, that the sky was a beneficent goddess who would stoop gently out of the infinite spaces and lift him to her breast, where he could lie amid the amber-fringed ruffles of cloud and look curiously down at the spinning ball of the earth? It might have beauty if he were far enough away to clear his nostrils of the stench of pain.

"It is funny," said the little doctor suddenly, "to think how much nearer we are, in state of mind, in everything, to the Germans than to anyone else."

"You mean that the soldiers in the trenches are all further from the people at home than from each other, no matter what side they are on."

The little doctor nodded.

"God, it's so stupid! Why can't we go over and talk to them? Nobody's fighting about

anything. . . . God, it's so hideously stupid!"
cried Martin, suddenly carried away, helpless in the flood of his passionate revolt.

"Life is stupid," said the little doctor sen-
tentiosuly.

Suddenly from the lines came a splutter of
machine-guns.

"Evensong!" cried the little doctor. "Ah,
but here's business. You'd better get your
car ready, my friend."

The brancardiers set the stretcher down at
the top of the steps that led to the door of the
dugout, so that Martin found himself looking
into the lean, sensitive face, stained a little
with blood about the mouth, of the wounded
man. His eyes followed along the shapeless
bundles of blood-flecked uniform till they
suddenly turned away. Where the middle of
the man had been, where had been the curved
belly and the genitals, where the thighs had
joined with a strong swerving of muscles to
the trunk, was a depression, a hollow pool of
blood, that glinted a little in the cold diffusion
of grey light from the west.

The rain beat hard on the window-panes of
the little room and hissed down the chimney
into the smouldering fire that set up thick

green smoke. At a plain oak table before the fireplace sat Martin Howe and Tom Randolph, Tom Randolph with his sunburned hands with their dirty nails spread flat and his head resting on the table between them, so that Martin could see the stiff black hair on top of his head and the dark nape of his neck going into shadow under the collar of the flannel shirt.

"Oh, God, it's too damned absurd! An arrangement for mutual suicide and no damned other thing," said Randolph, raising his head.

"A certain jolly asinine grotesqueness, though. I mean, if you were God and could look at it like that . . . Oh, Randy, why do they enjoy hatred so?"

"A question of taste . . . as the lady said when she kissed the cow."

"But it isn't. It isn't natural for people to hate that way, it can't be. It even disgusts the perfectly stupid damn-fool people, like Higgins, who believes that the Bible was written in God's own handwriting and that the newspapers tell the truth."

"It makes me sick at ma stomach, Howe, to talk to one of those hun-hatin' women, if they're male or female."

"It is a stupid affair, la vie, as the doctor at P.1. said yesterday. . . ."

"Hell, yes. . . ."

They sat silent, watching the rain beat on the window, and run down in sparkling finger-like streams.

"What I can't get over is these French women." Randolph threw back his head and laughed. "They're so bloody frank. Did I tell you about what happened to me at that last village on the Verdun road?"

"No."

"I was lyin' down for a nap under a plum-tree, a wonderfully nice place near a li'l brook an' all, an' suddenly that crazy Jane . . . You know the one that used to throw stones at us out of that broken-down house at the corner of the road . . . Anyway, she comes up to me with a funny look in her eyes an' starts makin' love to me. I had a regular wrastlin' match gettin' away from her."

"Funny position for you to be in, getting away from a woman."

"But doesn't that strike you funny? Why down where I come from a drunken mulatto woman wouldn't act like that. They all keep up a fake of not wantin' your attentions." His black eyes sparkled, and he laughed his deep

ringing laugh, that made the withered woman
smile as she set an omelette before them.

"Voilà, messieurs," she said with a grand
air, as if it were a boar's head that she was
serving.

Three French infantrymen came into the
café, shaking the rain off their shoulders.

"Nothing to drink but champagne at four
francs fifty," shouted Howe. "Dirty night
out, isn't it?"

"We'll drink that, then!"

Howe and Randolph moved up and they
all sat at the same table.

"Fortune of war?"

"Oh, the war, what do you think of the
war?" cried Martin.

"What do you think of the peste? You
think about saving your skin."

"What's amusing about us is that we three
have all saved our skin together," said one of
the Frenchmen.

"Yes. We are of the same class," said another, holding up his thumb. "Mobilised same
day." He held up his first finger. "Same
company." He held up a second finger.
"Wounded by the same shell. . . . Réformé
to the same depot behind the lines."

"Did'nt all marry the same girl, did you, to

make it complete?" asked Randolph.

They all shouted with laughter until the glasses along the bar rang.

"You must be Athos, Porthos, and d'Artagnan."

"We are," they shouted.

"Some more champagne, madame, for the three musketeers," sang Randolph in a sort of operatic yodle.

"All I have left is this," said the withered woman, setting a bottle down on the table.

"Is that poison?"

"It's cognac, it's very good cognac," said the old woman seriously.

"C'est du cognac! Vive le roi cognac! " everybody shouted.

> *"Au plein de mon cognac*
> *Qu'il fai bon, fait bon, fait bon,*
> *Au plein de mon cognac*
> *Qu'il fait bon dormir."*

"Down with the war! Who can sing the 'Internationale'?"

"Not so much noise, I beg you, gentlemen," came the withered woman's whining voice. "It's after hours. Last week I was fined. Next time I'll be closed up."

The night was black when Martin and Randolph, after lengthy and elaborate fare-

wells, started down the muddy road towards
the hospital. They staggered along the slip-
pery footpath beside the road, splashed every
instant with mud by camions, huge and dark,
that roared grindingly by. They ran and
skipped arm-in-arm and shouted at the top
of their lungs:

> *"Auprès de ma blonde,*
> *Qu'il fait bon, fait bon, fait bon,*
> *Auprès de ma blonde,*
> *Qu'il fait bon dormir."*

A stench of sweat and filth and formalde-
hyde caught them by the throat as they went
into the hospital tent, gave them a sense of
feverish bodies of men stretched all about
them, stirring in pain.

"A car for la Bassée, Ambulance 4," said
the orderly.

Howe got himself up off the hospital
stretcher, shoving his flannel shirt back into
his breeches, put on his coat and belt and felt
his way to the door, stumbling over the legs
of sleeping brancardiers as he went. Men
swore in their sleep and turned over heavily.
At the door he waited a minute, then shouted:

"Coming, Tom?"

"To damn sleepy," came Randolph's voice from under a blanket.

"I've got cigarettes, Tom. I'll smoke 'em all up if you don't come."

"All right, I'll come."

"Less noise, name of God!" cried a man, sitting up on his stretcher.

After the hospital, smelling of chloride and blankets and reeking clothes, the night air was unbelievably sweet. Like a gilt fringe on a dark shawl, a little band of brightness had appeared in the east.

"Some dawn, Howe, ain't it?"

As they were going off, their motor chugging regularly, an orderly said:

"It's a special case. Go for orders to the commandant."

Colours formed gradually out of chaotic grey as the day brightened. At the dressing-station an attendant ran up to the car.

"Oh, you're for the special case? Have you anything to tie a man with?"

"No, why?"

"It's nothing. He just tried to stab the sergeant-major."

The attendant raised a fist and tapped on his head as if knocking on a door. "It's nothing. He's quieter now."

"What caused it?"

"Who knows? There is so much. . . . He says he must kill everyone. . . . "

"Are you ready?"

A lieutenant of the medical corps came to the door and looked out. He smiled reassuringly at Martin Howe. "He's not violent any more. And we'll send two guardians."

A sergeant came out with a little packet which he handed to Martin.

"That's his. Will you give it to them at the hospital at Fourreaux? And here's his knife. They can give it back to him when he gets better. He has an idea he ought to kill everyone he sees. . . . Funny idea."

The sun had risen and shone gold across the broad rolling lands, so that the hedges and the poplar-rows cast long blue shadows over the fields. The man, with a guardian on either side of him who cast nervous glances to the right and to the left, came placidly, eyes straight in front of him, out of the dark interior of the dressing-station. He was a small man with moustaches and small, good-natured lips puffed into an o-shape. At the car he turned and saluted.

"Good-bye, my lieutenant. Thank you for your kindness," he said.

"Good-bye, old chap," said the lieutenant.
The little man stood up in the car, looking
about him anxiously.

"I've lost my knife. Where's my knife?"
The guards got in behind him with a nervous, sheepish air. They answered reassuringly, "The driver's got it. The American's
go it."

"Good."
The orderly jumped on the seat with the
two Americans to show the way. He whispered in Martin's ear:

"He's crazy. He says that to stop the war
you must kill everybody, kill everybody."

In an open valley that sloped between hills
covered with beech-woods, stood the tall abbey, a Gothic nave and apse with beautifully
traced windows, with the ruin of a very
ancient chapel on one side, and crossing the
back, a well-proportioned Renaissance building that had been a dormitory. The first
time that Martin saw the abbey, it towered in
ghostly perfection above a low veil of mist
that made the valley seem a lake in the shin-
ing moonlight. The lines were perfectly
quiet, and when he stopped the motor of his
ambulance, he could hear the wind rustling

among the beech-woods. Except for the dirty smell of huddled soldiers that came now and then in drifts along with the cool wood-scents, there might have been no war at all. In the soft moonlight the great traceried windows and the buttresses and the high-pitched roof seemed as gorgeously untroubled by decay as if the carvings on the cusps and arches had just come from under the careful chisel of the Gothic workmen.

"And you say we've progressed," he whispered to Tom Randolph.

"God, it is fine."

They wandered up and down the road a long time, silently, looking at the tall apse of the abbey, breathing the cool night air, moist with mist, in which now and then was the huddled, troubling smell of soldiers. At last the moon, huge and swollen with gold, set behind the wooded hills, and they went back to the car, where they rolled up in their blankets and went to sleep.

Behind the square lantern that rose over the crossing, there was a trap door in the broken tile roof, from which you could climb to the observation post in the lantern. Here, half on the roof and half on the platform behind the trap-door, Martin would spend the

long summer afternoons when there was no
call for the ambulance, looking at the Gothic
windows of the lantern and the blue sky beyond, where huge soft clouds passed slowly
over, darkening the green of the woods and
of the weed-grown fields of the valley with
their moving shadows.

There was almost no activity on that part
of the front. A couple of times a day a few
snapping discharges would come from the
seventy-fives of the battery behind the Abbey,
and the woods would resound like a shaken
harp as the shells passed over to explode on
the crest of the hill that blocked the end of
the valley where the Boches were.

Martin would sit and dream of the quiet
lives the monks must have passed in their
beautiful abbey so far away in the Forest of
the Argonne, digging and planting in the rich
lands of the valley, making flowers bloom in
the garden, of which traces remained in the
huge beds of sunflowers and orange marigolds
that bloomed along the walls of the dormitory.
In a room in the top of the house he had found
a few torn remnants of books; there must
have been a library in the old days, rows and
rows of musty-smelling volumes in rich brown
calf worn by use to a velvet softness, and in

cream-coloured parchment where the finger-marks of generations showed brown; huge psalters with notes and chants illuminated in green and ultramarine and gold; manuscripts out of the Middle Ages with strange script and pictures in pure vivid colours; lives of saints, thoughts polished by years of quiet meditation of old divines; old romances of chivalry; tales of blood and death and love where the crude agony of life was seen through a dawnlike mist of gentle beauty.

"God! if there were somewhere nowadays where you could flee from all this stupidity, from all this cant of governments, and this hideous reiteration of hatred, this strangling hatred . . ." he would say to himself, and see himself working in the fields, copying parchments in quaint letterings, drowsing his feverish desires to calm in the deep-throated passionate chanting of the endless offices of the Church.

One afternoon towards evening as he lay on the tiled roof with his shirt open so that the sun warmed his throat ad chest, half asleep in the beauty of the building and of the woods and the clouds that drifted over-head, he heard a strain from the organ in the church: a few deep notes in broken rhythm that filled him with wonder, as if he had suddenly been transported back to the quiet days of the monks. The rhythm changed in an instant, and through the squeakiness of shattered pipes came a swirl of fake-oriental ragtime that resounded like mocking laughter in the old vaults and arches. He went down into the church and found Tom Randolph playing on the little organ, pumping desperately with his feet.

"Hello! Impiety I call it; putting your lustful tunes into that pious old organ."

"I bet the ole monks had a merry time, lecherous ole devils," said Tom, playing away.

"If there were monasteries nowadays," said Martin, "I think I'd go into one."

"But there are. I'll end up in one, most like, if they don't put me in jail first. I reckon every living soul would be a candidate for either one if it'd get them out of this God-damned war."

There was a shriek overhead that reverberated strangely in the vaults of the church and made the swallows nesting there fly in and out through the glassless windows. Tom Randolph stopped on a wild chord.

"Guess they don't like me playin'."

"That one didn't explode though."

"That one did, by gorry," said Randolph, getting up off the floor, where he had thrown himself automatically. A shower of tiles came rattlin~ off the roof, and through the noise could be heard the fightened squeaking of the swallows.

"I am afraid that winged somebody."

"They must have got wind of the ammunition dump in the cellar."

"Hell of a place to put a dressing-station—over an ammunition dump!"

The whitewashed room used as a dressing-station had a smell of blood stronger than the chloride. A doctor was leaning over a stretcher on which Martin caught a glimpse of two naked legs with flecks of blood on the white skin, as he passed through on his way to the car.

"Three stretcher-cases for Les Islettes. Very softly," said the attendant, handing him the papers.

Jolting over the shell-pitted road, the car wound slowly through unploughed weed-grown fields. At every jolt came a rasping groan from the wounded men.

As they came back towards the front posts again, they found all the batteries along the road firing. The air was a chaos of explosions that jabbed viciously into their ears, above the reassuring purr of the motor. Nearly to the abbey a soldier stopped them.

"Put the car behind the trees and get into a dugout. They're shelling the abbey."

As he spoke a whining shriek grew suddenly loud over their heads. The soldier threw himself flat in the muddy road. The explosion brought gravel about their ears and made a curious smell of almonds.

Crowded in the door of the dugout in the hill opposite they watched the abbey as shell after shell tore through the roof or exploded in the strong buttresses of the apse. Dust rose high above the roof and filled the air with an odour of damp tiles and plaster. The woods resounded in a jangling tremor, with the batteries that started firing one after the other.

"God, I hate them for that!" said Randolph between his teeth.

"What do you want? It's an observation post."

"I know, but damn it!"

There was a series of explosions; a shell fragment whizzed past their heads.

"It's not safe there. You'd better come in

all the way," someone shouted from within the dugout.

"I want to see; damn it.. . . I'm goin' to stay and see it out, Howe. That place meant a hell of a lot to me." Randolph blushed as he spoke.

Another bunch of shells crashing so near together they did not hear the scream. When the cloud of dust blew away, they saw that the lantern had fallen in on the roof of the apse, leaving only one wall and the tracery of a window, of which the shattered carving stood out cream-white against the reddish evening sky.

There was a lull in the firing. A few swallows still wheeled about the walls, giving shrill little cries.

They saw the flash of a shell against the sky as it exploded in the part of the tall roof that still remained. The roof crumpled and fell in, and again dust hid the abbey.

"Oh, I hate this!" said Tom Randolph. "But the question is, what's happened to our grub? The popote is buried four feet deep in Gothic art. . . . Damn fool idea, putting a dressing-station over an ammunition dump."

"Is the car hit?" The orderly came up to them.

"Dont' think so."

"Good. Four stretcher-cases for 42 at once."

At night in a dugout. Five men playing cards about a lamp-flame that blows from one side to the other in the gusty wind that puffs every now and then down the mouth of the dugout and whirls round it like something alive trying to beat a way out.

Each time the lamp blows the shadows of the five heads writhe upon the corrugated tin ceiling. In the distance, like kettle-drums beaten for a dance, a constant reverberation of guns.

Martin Howe, stretched out in the straw of one of the bunks, watches their faces in the flickering shadows. He wishes he had the patience to play too. No, perhaps it is better to look on; it would be so silly to be killed in the middle of one of those grand gestures one makes in slamming the card down that takes the trick. Suddenly he thinks of all the lives that must, in these last three years, have ended in that grand gesture. It is too silly. He seems to see their poor lacerated souls, clutching their greasy dogeared cards, climb to a squalid Valhalla, and there, in tobacco-stinking rooms, like those of the little cafés behind the lines, sit in groups of five, shuffling, dealing, taking tricks, always with the same slam of the cards on the table, pausing now and then to scratch their louse-eaten flesh.

At this moment, how many men, in all the long Golgotha that stretches from Belfort to the sea, must be trying to cheat their boredom and their misery with that grand gesture of slamming the cards down to take a trick, while in their ears, like tom-toms, pounds the death-dance of the guns.

Martin lies on his back looking up at the curved corrugated ceiling of the dugout, where the shadows of the five heads writhe in fantastic shapes. Is it death they are playing, that they are so merry when they take a trick?

CHAPTER V

THE three planes gleamed like mica in the intense blue of the sky. Round about the shrapnel burst in little puffs like cotton-wool. A shout went up from the soldiers who stood in groups in the street of the ruined town. A whistle split the air, followed by a rending snort that tailed off into the moaning of a wounded man.

"By damn, they're nervy. They dropped a bomb."

"I should say they did."

"The dirty bastards, to get a fellow who's going on permission. Now if they beaded you on the way back you wouldn't care."

In the sky an escadrille of French planes had appeared and the three German specks had vanished, followed by a trail of little puffs of shrapnel. The indigo dome of the afternoon sky was full of a distant snoring of motors.

The train screamed outside the station and the permissionaires ran for the platform, their packed musettes bouncing at their hips.

FIRST ENCOUNTER

The dark boulevards, with here and there a blue lamp lighting up a bench and a few treetrunks, or a faint glow from inside a closed café where a boy in shirt-sleeves is sweeping the floor. Crowds of soldiers, Belgians, Americans, Canadians, civilians with canes and straw hats and well-dressed women on their arms, shopgirls in twos and threes laughing with shrill merry voices; and everywhere girls of the street, giggling alluringly in hoarse, dissipated tones, clutching the arms of drunken soldiers, tilting themselves temptingly in men's way as they walk along. Cigarettes and cigars make spots of reddish light, and now and then a match lighted makes a man's face stand out in yellow relief and glints red in the eyes of people round about.

Drunk with their freedom, with the jangle of voices, with the rustle of trees in the faint light, with the scents of women's hair and cheap perfumes, Howe and Randolph stroll along slowly, down one side to the shadowy columns of the Madeleine, where a few flower-women still offer roses, scenting the darkness, then back again past the Opéra towards the Porte St. Martin, lingering to look in the offered faces of women, to listen to snatches of talk, to chatter laughingly with girls who squeeze their arms with impatience.

"I'm goin' to find the prettiest girl in Paris, and then you'll see the dust fly, Howe, old man."

The hors d'oeuvre came on a circular three-tiered stand; red strips of herrings and silver anchovies, salads where green peas and bits of carrot lurked under golden layers of sauce, sliced tomatoes, potato salad green-specked with parsley, hard-boiled eggs barely visible under thickness of vermilion-tinged dressing, olives, radishes, discs of sausage of many different forms and colours, complicated bundles of spiced salt fish, and, forming the apex, a fat terra-cotta jar of paté de foie gras. Howe poured out pale-coloured Chablis.

"I used to think that down home was the only place they knew how to live, but oh, boy . . ." said Tom Randolph, breaking a little loaf of bread that made a merry crackling sound.

"It's worth starving to death on singe and pinard for four months."

After the hors d'oeuvre had been taken away, leaving them Rabelaisianly gay, with a joyous sense of orgy, came sole hidden in a cream-coloured sauce with mussels in it.

"After the war, Howe, ole man, let's riot all over Europe; I'm getting a taste for this sort of livin'."

"You can play the fiddle, can't you, Tom?"

"Enough to scrape out "Auprès de ma blonde" on a bet."

"Then we'll wander about and you can support me. . . . Or else I'll dress as a monkey and you can fiddle and I'll gather the pennies."

"By gum, that'd be great sport."

"Look, we must have some red wine with the veal."

"Let's have Macon."

"All the same to me as long as there's plenty of it."

Their round table with its white cloth and its bottles of wine and its piles of ravished artichoke leaves was the centre of a noisy, fantastic world. Ever since the orgy of the hors d'oevres things had been evolving to grotesqueness, faces, whites of eyes, twisted red of lips, crow-like forms of waiters, colours of hats and uniforms, all involved and jumbled in the melée of talk and clink and clatter.

The red hand of the waiter pouring the Chartreuse, green like a stormy sunset, into

small glasses before them broke into the vivid
imaginatings that had been unfolding in their
talk through dinner. No, they had been saying, it could not go on; some day amid the
rending crash of shells and the whine of
shrapnel fragments, people everywhere, in
all uniforms, in trenches, packed in camions,
in stretchers, in hospitals, crowded behind
guns, involved in telephone apparatus, gen-
erals at their dinner-tables, colonels sipping
liqueurs, majors developing photographs,
would jump to their feet and bust out laughing at the solemn inanity, at the stupid, vicious
pomposity of what they were doing. Laughter
would untune the sky. It would be a new
progress of Bacchus. Drunk with laughter
at the sudden vision of the silliness of the
world, officers, and soldiers, prisoners working on the roads, deserters being driven towards the trenches would throw down their
guns and their spades and their heavy packs,
and start marching, or driving in artillery
waggons or in camions, staff cars, private
trains, towards their capitals, where they
would laugh the deputies, the senators, the
congressmen, the M.P.'s out of their chairs,
laugh the presidents and the prime ministers,
and kaisers and dictators out of their plush-

carpeted offices; the sun would wear a broad
grin and would whisper the joke to the moon,
who would giggle and ripple with it all night
long. . . . The red hand of the waiter, with
thick nails and work-swollen knuckles, poured
Chartreuse into the small glasses before them.

"That," said Tom Randolph, when he had
half finished his liqueur, is the girl for me."

"But, Tom, she's with a French officer."

"They're fighting like cat and dogs. You
can see that, can't you?"

"Yes," agreed Howe vaguely.

"Pay the bill. I'll meet you at the corner
of the boulevard." Tom Randolph was out
of the door. The girl, who had a little of the
aspect of a pierrot, with dark skin and bright
lips and gold-yellow hat and dress, and the
sour-looking officer who was with her, were
getting up to go.

At the corner of the Boulevard Howe heard
a woman's voice joining with Randolph's rich
laugh.

"What did I tell you? They split at the
door and here we are, Howe. . . . Mademoi-
selle Montreuil, let me introduce a friend.
Look, before it's too late, we must have a
drink."

At the café table next to them an Englishman was seated with his head sunk on his
chest.

"Oh, I say, you woke me up."

"Sorry."

"No harm. Jolly good thing."

They invited him over to their table. There
was a moist look about his eyes and a thickness to his voice that denoted alcohol.

"You mustn't mind me. I'm forgetting.
. . . I've been doing it for a week. This is
the first leave I've had in eighteen months.
You Canadians?"

"No. Ambulance service; Americans."

"New at the game then. You're lucky. . . .
Before I left the front I saw a man tuck a
hand-grenade under the pillow of a poor
devil of a German prisoner. The prisoner
said, 'Thank you.' The grenade blew him to
hell! God! Know anywhere you can get
whisky in this bloody town?"

"We'll have to hurry; it's near closing-
time."

"Right-o."

They started off, Randolph and the girl
talking intimately, their heads close together,
Martin supporting the Englishman.

"I need a bit o' whisky to put me on my pins"

They tumbled into the seats round a table at an American bar.

The Englishman felt in his pocket.

"Oh, I say," he cried, "I've got a ticket to the theatre. It's a box. . . . We can all get in. Come along; let's hurry."

They walked a long while, blundering through the dark streets, and at last stopped at a blue-lighted door.

"Here it is; push in."

"But there are two gentlemen and a lady already in the box, meester."

"No matter, there'll be room." The Englishman waved the ticket in the air.

The little round man with a round red face. who was taking the tickets stuttered in bad English and then dropped into French. Meanwhile, the whole party had filed in, leaving the Englishman, who kept waving the ticket in the little man's face.

Two gendarmes, the theatre guards, came up menacingly; the Englishman's face wreathed itself in smiles; he linked an arm in each of the gendarmes', and pushed them towards the bar.

"Come drink to the Entente Cordiale. . . .

Vive la France!"

In the box were two Australians and a woman who leaned her head on the chest of one and then the other alternately, laughing so that you could see the gold caps in her black teeth.

They were annoyed at the intrusion that packed the box insupportably tight, so that the woman had to sit on the men's laps, but the air soon cleared in laughter that caused people in the orchestra to stare angrily at the box full of noisy men in khaki. At last the Englishman came, squeezing himself in with a finger mysteriously on his lips. He plucked at Martin's arm, a serious set look coming suddenly over his grey eyes. "It was like this"—his breath laden with whisky was like a halo round Martin's head—"the Hun was a nice little chap, couldn't 'a' been more than eighteen; had a shoulder broken and he thought that my pal was fixing the pillow. He said 'Thank you' with a funny German accent. . . . Mind you, he said 'Thank you'; that's what hurt. And the man laughed. God damn him, he laughed when the poor devil said 'Thank you.' And the grenade blew him to hell."

The stage was a glare of light in Martin's

eyes; he felt as he had when at home he had leaned over and looked straight into the headlight of an auto drawn up to the side of the road. Screening him from the glare were the backs of people's heads: Tom Randolph's head and his girl's, side by side, their cheeks touching, the pointed red chin of one of the Australians and the frizzy hair of the other woman.

In the entr'acte they all stood at the bar, where it was very hot and an orchestra was playing and there were many men in khaki in all stages of drunkenness, being led about by women who threw jokes at each other behind the men's backs.

"Here's to mud," said one of the Australians. 'The war'll end when everybody is drowned in mud."

The orchestra began playing the "Madelon" and everyone roared out the marching song that, worn threadbare as it was, still had a roistering verve to it that caught people's blood.

People had gone back for the last act. The two Australians, the Englishman, and the two Americans still stood talking.

"Mind you, I'm not what you'd call susceptible. I'm not soft. I got over all that long ago." The Englishman was addressing the company in general. "But the poor beggar said 'Thank you'."

"What's he saying?" asked a woman, plucking at Martin's arm.

"He's telling about a German atrocity."

"Oh, the dirty Germans! What things they've done!" the woman answered mechanically.

Somehow, during the entr'acte, the Australians had collected another woman; and a strange fat woman with lips painted very small, and very large bulging eyes, had attached herself to Martin. He suffered her because every time he looked at her she burst out laughing.

The bar was closing. They had a drink of champagne all around that made the fat woman give little shrieks of delight. They drifted towards the door, and stood, a formless, irresolute group, in the dark street in front of the theatre.

Randolph came up to Martin.

"Look. We're goin'. I wonder if I ought to leave my money with you . . ."

"I doubt if I'm a safe person to-night . . ."

"All right. I'll take it along. Look . . . let's meet for breakfast"

"At the 'Café de la Paix'."

"All right. If she is nice I'll bring her."

"She looks charming."

Tom Randolph pressed Martin's hand and was off. There was a sound of a kiss in the darkness.

"I say, I've got to have something to eat," said the Englishman. ' 'I didn't have a bit of dinner. I say—mangai, mangai." He made gestures of puttings things into his mouth in the direction of the fat woman.

The three women put their heads together. One of them knew a place, but it was a dreadful place. Really, they mustn't think that . . . She only knew it because when she was very young a man had taken her there who wanted to seduce her.

At that everyone laughed and the voices of the women rose shrill.

"All right, don't talk; let's go there," said one of the Australians. 'We'll atttend to the seducing."

A thick woman, a tall comb in the back of her high-piled black hair, and an immovable face with jaw muscled like a prize-fighter's, served them with cold chicken and ham and champagne in a room with mouldering greenish wall-paper lighted by a red-shaded lamp.

The Australians ate and sang and made love to their women. The Englishman went to sleep with his head on the table.

Martin leaned back out of the circle of light, keeping up a desultory conversation with the woman beside him, listening to the sounds of the men's voices down corridors, of the front door being opened and slammed again and again, and of forced, shrill giggles of women.

"Unfortunately, I have an engagement to-night," said Martin to the woman beside him, whose large spherical breasts heaved as she talked, and who rolled herself nearer to him invitingly, seeming with her round pop-eyes and her round cheeks to be made up entirely of small spheres and large soft ones.

"Oh, but it is too late. You can break it."

"It's at four o'clock."

"Then we have time, ducky."

"It's something really romantic, you see."

"The young are always lucky." She rolled her eyes in sympathetic admiration. "This will be the fourth night this week that I have not made a sou. . . . I'll chuck myself into the river soon."

Martin felt himself softening towards her. He slipped a twenty-franc note in her hand.

"Oh, you are too good. You are really gallant homme, you."

Martin buried his face in his hands, dreaming of the woman he would like to love tonight. She should be very dark, with red lips and stained cheeks, like Randolph's girl; she should have small breasts and slender, dark, dancer's thighs, and in her arms he could forget everything but the madness and the mystery and the intricate life of Paris about them. He thought of Montmartre, and Louise in the opera standing at her window singing the madness of Paris. . . .

One of the Australians had gone away with a little woman in a pink negligée. The other Australian and the Englishman were standing unsteadily near the table, each supported by a sleepy-looking girl. Leaving the fat woman sadly finishing the remains of the chicken, large tears rolling from her eyes, they left the house and walked for a long time down dark streets, three men and two women, the Englishman being supported in the middle, singing in a desultory fashion.

They stopped under a broken sign of black

letters on greyish glass, within which one
feeble electric light bulb made a red glow.
The pavement was wet, and glimmered where
it slanted up to the lamp-post at the next
corner.

"Here we are. Come along, Janey," cried
the Australian in a brisk voice.

The door opened and slammed again.
Martin and the other girl stood on the pavement facing each other. The Englishman col-
lapsed on the doorstep, and began to snore.

"Well, there's only you and me," she said.

"Oh, if you were only a person, instead of
being a member of a profession——" said
Martin softly.

"Come," she said.

"No, dearie. I must go," said Martin.

"As you will. I'll take care of your friend."
She yawned.

He kissed her and strode down the dark
street, his nostrils full of the smell of the
rouge on her lips.

He walked a long while with his hat off,
breathing deep of the sharp night air. The
streets were black and silent. Intemperate
desires prowled like cats in the darkness.

He woke up and stretched himself stiffly,

smelling grass and damp earth. A pearly lavender mist was all about him, through which loomed the square towers of Notre Dame and the row of kings across the facade and the sculpture about the darkness of the doorways. He had lain down on his back on the little grass plot of the Parvis Notre Dame to look at the stars, and had fallen asleep.

It must be nearly dawn. Words were droning importunately in his head. "The poor beggar said 'Thank you' with a funny German accent and the grenade blew him to hell." He remembered the man he had once helped to pick up in whose pocket a grenade had exploded. Before that he had not realised that torn flesh was such a black-red, like sausage meat.

"Get up, you can't lie there," cried a gendarme

"Notre Dame is beautiful in the morning," said Martin, stepping across the low rail on to the pavement.

"Ah, yes; it is beautiful."

Martin Howe sat on the rail of the bridge and looked. Before him, with nothing distinct yet to be seen, were two square towers and the tracery between them and the row of kings on the facade, and the long series of flying buttresses of the flank, gleaming through the mist, and, barely visible, the dark, slender spire soaring above the crossing. So had the abbey in the forest gleamed tall in the misty moonlight; like mist, only drab and dense, the dust had risen above the tall apse as the shells tore it to pieces.

Amid a smell of new-roasted coffee he sat at a table and watched people pass briskly through the ruddy sunlight. Waiters in shirtsleeves were rubbing off the other tables and putting out the chairs. He sat sipping coffee, feeling languid and nerveless. After a while Tom Randolph, looking very young and brown with his hat a little on one side, came along. With him, plainly dressed in blue serge, was the girl. They sat down and she dropped her head on his shoulder, covering her eyes with her dark lashes.

"Oh, I am so tired."

"Poor child! You must go home and go back to bed."

"But I've got to go to work."

"Poor thing." They kissed each other tenderly and languidly.

The waiter came with coffee and hot milk and little crisp loaves of bread.

"Oh, Paris is wonderful in the early morning!" said Martin.

"Indeed it is. . . . Good-bye little girl, if you must go. We'll see each other again."

"You must call me Yvonne" She pouted a little.

"All right, Yvonne." He got to his feet and pressed her two hands.

"Well, what sort of a time did you have, Howe?"

"Curious. I lost our friends one by one, left two women and slept a little while on the grass in front of Notre Dame. That was my real love of the night."

"My girl was charming. . . . Honestly, I'd marry her in a minute." He laughed a merry laugh.

"Let's take a cab somewhere."

They climbed into a victoria and told the driver to go to the Madeleine.

"Look, before I do anthing else I must go to the hotel."

"Why?"

"Preventives."

"Of course; you'd better go at once."

The cab rattled merrily along the streets

JOHN DOS PASSOS

where the early sunshine cast rust patches on the grey houses and on the thronged fantastic chimney-pots that rose in clusters and hedges from the mansard roofs.

CHAPTER VI

THE lamp in the hut of the road control casts an oblong of light on the white wall opposite. The patch of light is constantly crossed and scalloped and obscured by shadows of rifles and helmets and packs of men passing. Now and then the shadow of a single man, a nose and a chin under a helmet, a head bent forward with the weight of the pack, or a pack alone beside which slants a rifle, shows up huge and fantastic with its loaf of bread and its pair of shoes and its pots and pans.

Then with a jingle of harness and clank of steel, train after train of artillery comes up out of the darkness of the road, is thrown by the lamp into vivid relief and is swallowed again by the blackness of the village street, short bodies of seventy-fives sticking like ducks' tails from between their large wheels; caisson after caisson of ammunition, huge waggons hooded and unhooded, filled with a chaos of equipment that catches fantastic lights and throws huge muddled shadows on the white wall of the house.

"Put that light out. Name of God, do you want to have them start chucking shells into here?" comes a voice shrill with anger. The brisk trot of the officer's horse is lost in the clangour.

The door of the hut slams to and only a thin ray of orange light penetrates into the blackness of the road, where with jungle of harness and clatter of iron and tramp of hoofs, gun after gun, caisson after caisson, waggon after waggon files by. Now and then the passing stops entirely and matches flare where men light pipes and cigarettes. Coming from the other direction with throbbing of motors, a convoy of camions, huge black oblongs, grinds down the other side of the road. Horses rear and there are shouts and curses and clacking of reins in the darkness.

Far away where the lowering clouds meet the hills beyond the village a white glare grows and fades again at intervals: starshells.

"There's a most tremendous concentration of sanitary sections."

"You bet; two American sections and a French one in this village; three more down the road. Something's up."

FIRST ENCOUNTER

"There's goin' to be an attack at St. Mihiel, a Frenchman told me."

"I heard that the Germans were concentrating for an offensive in the Four de Paris."

"Damned unlikely."

"Anyway, this is the third week we've been in this bloody hole with our feet in the mud."

"They've got us quartered in a barn with a regular brook flowing through the middle of it."

"The main thing about this damned war is ennui — just plain boredom."

"Not forgetting the mud."

Three ambulance drivers in slickers were on the front seat of a car. The rain fell in perpendicular sheets, pattering on the roof of the car and on the puddles that filled the village street. Streaming with water, blackened walls of ruined houses rose opposite them above a rank growth of weeds. Beyond were rain-veiled hills. Every little while, slithering through the rain, splashing mud to the right and left, a convoy of camions went by and disappeared, truck after truck, in the white streaming rain.

Inside the car Tom Randolph was playing an accordion, letting nostalgic little songs filter out amid the hard pattern of the rain.

"Oh, I's been workin' on de railroad
  All de livelong day;
I's been workin' on de railroad
  Jus' to pass de time away."

The men on the front seat leaned back and shook the water off their knees and hummed the song.

The accordion had stopped. Tom Randolph was lying on his back on the floor of the car with his arm over his eyes. The rain fell endlessly, rattling on the roof of the car, dancing silver in the coffee-coloured puddles of the road. Their boredom fell into the rhythm of crooning self-pity of the old coon song:

"I's been workin' on de railroad
  All de livelong day;
I's been workin' on de railroad
  Jus' to pass de time away."

"Oh God, something's got to happen soon."

Lost in rubber boots, and a huge gleaming slicker and hood, the section leader splashed across the road.

"All cars must be ready to leave at six to-night."

"Yay. Where we goin'?"

"Orders haven't come yet. We're to be in readiness to leave at six to-night. . . ."

"I tell you, fellers, there's goin' to be an attack. This concentration of sanitary sections means something. You can't tell me . . ."

"They say they have beer," said the aspirant behind Martin in the long line of men who waited in the hot sun for the copé to open, while the dust the staff cars and camions raised as they whirred by on the road settled in a blanket over the village.

"Cold beer?"

"Of course not," said the aspirant, laughing so that all the brilliant ivory teeth showed behind his red lips. "It'll be detestable. I'm getting it because it's rare, for sentimental reasons."

Martin laughed, looking in the man's brown face, a face in which all past expressions seemed to linger in the fine lines about the mouth and eyes and in the modelling of the cheeks and temples.

"You don't understand that," said the aspirant again.

"Indeed I do."

Later they sat on the edge of the stone wellhead in the courtyard behind the store, drinking warm beer out of tin cups blackened by wine, and staring at a tall barn that had crumpled at one end so that it looked, with its two frightened little square windows, like a cow kneeling down.

"Is it true that the ninety-second's going up to the lines to-night?"

"Yes ,we're going up to make a little attack. Probably I'll come back in your little omnibus."

"I hope you won't."

"I'd be very glad to. A lucky wound! But I'll probably be killed. This is the first time I've gone up to the front that I didn't expect to be killed. So it'll probably happen."

Martin Howe could not help looking at him suddenly. The aspirant sat at ease on the stone margin of the well, leaning against the wrought iron support for the bucket, one knee clasped in his strong, heavily-veined hands. Dead he would be different. Martin's mind could hardly grasp the connection between this man full of latent energies, full of thoughts and desires, this man whose shoulder he would have liked to have put his arm round from friendliness, with whom he would have liked to go for long walks, with whom he would have liked to sit long into the night drinking and talking — and those huddled, pulpy masses of blue uniform half-buried in the mud of ditches.

"Have you ever seen a herd of cattle being driven to an abattoir on a fine May morning?" asked the aspirant in a scornful, jaunty tone, as if he had guessed Martin's thoughts.

"I wonder what they think of it."

"It's not that I'm resigned. . . . Don't think that. Resignation is too easy. That's why the herd can be driven by a boy of six . . . or a prime minister!"

Martin was sitting with his arms crossed. The fingers of one hand were squeezing the muscles of his forearm. It gave him pleasure to feel the smooth, firm modelling of his arm through his sleeve. And how would that feel when it was dead, when a steel splinter had slithered through it? A momentary stench of putrefaction filled his nostrils, making his stomach contract with nausea.

"I'm not resigned either," he shouted in a laugh. "I am going to do something some day, but first I must see. I want to be initiated in all the circles of hell."

"I'd play the part of Virgil pretty well," said the aspirant, "but I suppose Virgil was a staff officer."

"I must go," said Martin. "My name's Martin Howe, S.S.U. 84."

"Oh yes, you are quartered in the square.

My name is Merrier. You'll probably carry me back in your little omnibus.

When Howe got back to where the cars were packed in a row in the village square, Randolph came to him and whispered in his ear:

"D.J.'s to-morrow."

"The attack. It's to-morrow at three in the morning; instructions are going to be given out to-night."

A detonation behind them was like a blow on the head, making their ear-drums ring. The glass in the headlight of one of the cars tinkled to the ground.

"The 410 behind the church, that was. Pretty near knocks the wind out of you."

"Say, Randolph, have you heard the new orders?"

"No."

A tall, fair-haired man came out from the front of his car where he had been working on the motor, holding his grease-covered hands away from him.

"It's put off," he said, lowering his voice mysteriously. "D.J.s not till day after tomorrow at four-twenty. But tomorrow we're going up to relieve the section that's coming out and take over the posts. They say it's hell up there. The Germans have a new gas that you can't smell at all. The other section's got about five men gassed, and a bunch of them have broken down. The posts are shelled all the time."

"Great," said Tom Randolph. "We'll see the real thing this time."

There was a whistling shriek overhead and all three of them fell in a heap on the ground in front of the car. There was a crash that echoed amid the house-walls, and a pillar of black smoke stood like a cypress tree at the other end of the village street.

"Talk about the real thing!" said Martin.

"Ole 410 evidently woke 'em up some."

It was the fifth time that day that Martin's car had passed the cross-roads where the calvary was. Someone had propped up the fallen crucifix so that it tilted dark despairing arms against the sunset sky where the sun gleamed like a huge copper kettle lost in its own steam. The rain made bright yellowish stripes across the sky and dripped from the cracked feet of the old wooden Christ, whose gaunt, scarred figure hung out from the tilted cross, swaying a little under the beating of the rain.

Martin was wiping the mud from his hands

after changing a wheel. He stared curiously at the fallen jowl and the cavernous eyes that had meant for some country sculptor ages ago the utterest agony of pain. Suddenly he noticed that where the crown of thorns had been about the forehead of the Christ some- one had wound barbed wire. He smiled, and asked the swaying figure in his mind:

"And You, what do You think of it?"

For an instant he could feel wire barbs ripping through his own flesh.

He leaned over to crank the car.

The road was filled suddenly with the tramp and splash of troops marching, their wet helmets and their rifles gleaming in the coppery sunset. Even through the clean rain came the smell of filth and sweat and misery of troops marching. The faces under the hel- mets were strained and colorless and cadav- erous from the weight of the equipment on their necks and their backs and their thighs. The faces drooped under the helmets, tilted to one side or the other, distorted and wooden like the face of the figure that dangled from the cross.

Above the splash of feet through mud and the jingle of equipment, came occasionally the ping, ping of shrapnel bursting at the next cross-roads at the edge of the woods.

Martin sat in the car with the motor racing, waiting for the end of the column.

One of the stragglers who floundered along through the churned mud of the road after the regular tanks had passed stopped still and looked up at the tilted cross. From the next cross-roads came, at intervals, the sharp twanging ping of shrapnel bursting.

The straggler suddenly began kicking feebly at the prop of the cross with his foot, and then dragged himself off after the column. The cross fell forward with a dull splintering splash into the mud of the road.

The road went down the hill in long zigzags, through a village at the bottom where out of the mist that steamed from the little river a spire with a bent weathercock rose above the broken roof of the church, then up the hill again into the woods. In the woods the road stretched green and gold in the first horizontal sunlight. Among the thick trees, roofs covered with branches, were rows of long portable barracks with doors decorated with rustic work. At one place a sign announced in letters made of wattled sticks, "Camp des Pommiers."

A few birds sang in the woods, and at a pump they passed a lot of men stripped to the waist who were leaning over washing, laughing and splashing in the sunlight. Every now and then, distant, metallic, the pong, pong, pong of a battery of seventy-fives resounded through the rustling trees.

"Looks like a camp meetin' ground in Georgia," said Tom Randolph, blowing his whistle to make two men carrying a large steaming pot on a pole between them get out of the way.

The road became muddier as they went deeper into the woods, and, turning into a cross-road, the car began slithering, skidding a little at the turns, through thick soupy mud. On either side the woods became broken and jagged, stumps and split boughs littering the ground, trees snapped off halfway up. In the air there was a scent of newly-split timber and of turned-up woodland earth, and among them a sweetish rough smell.

Covered with greenish mud, splashing the mud right and left with their great flat wheels, camions began passing them returning from the direction of the lines.

At last at a small red cross flag they stopped and ran the car into a grove of tall chestnuts, where they parked it beside another car of their section and lay down among the crisp leaves, listening to occasional shells whining far overhead. All through the wood was a continuous ping, pong, ping of batteries, with the crash of a big gun coming now and then like the growl of a bull-frog among the sing-song of small toads in a pond at night.

Through the trees from where they lay they could see the close-packed wooden crosses of a cemetery from which came a sound of spaded earth, and where, preceded by a priest in a muddy cassock, little two-wheeled carts piled with shapeless things in sacks kept being brought up and unloaded and dragged away again.

Showing alternately dark and light in the sun and shadow of the woodland road, a cook waggon, short chimney giving out blue smoke, and cauldrons steaming, clatters ahead of Martin and Randolph; the backs of two men in heavy blue coats, their helmets showing above the narrow driver's seat. On either side of the road short yellow flames keep spitting up, slanting from hidden guns amid a pandemonium of noise.

Up the road a sudden column of black

smoke rises among falling trees. A louder explosion and the cook waggon in front of them vanishes in a new whirl of thick smoke. Accelerator pressed down, the car plunges along the rutted road, tips, and a wheel sinks in the new shell-hole. The hind wheels spin for a moment, spattering gravel about, and just as another roar comes behind them, bite into the road again and the car goes on, speeding through the alternate sun and shadow of the woods. Martin remembers the beating legs of a mule rolling on its back on the side of the road and, steaming in the fresh morning air, the purple and yellow and red of its ripped belly.

"Did you get the smell of almonds? I sort of like it," says Randolph, drawing a long breath as the car slowed down again.

The woods at night, fantastic blackness full of noise and yellow leaping flames from the mouths of guns. Now and then the sulphurous flash of a shell explosion and the sound of trees falling and shell fragments swishing through the air. At intervals over a little knoll in the direction of the trenches, a white star-shell falls slowly, making the trees and the guns among their tangle of hiding branches cast long green-black shadows, drowning the wood in a strange glare of desolation.

"Where the devil's the abri?"

Everything drowned in the detonations of three guns, one after the other, so near as to puff hot air in their faces in the midst of the blinding concussion.

"Look, Tom, this is foolish; the abri's right here."

"I haven't got it in my pocket, Howe. Damn those guns."

Again everything is crushed in the concussion of the guns.

They throw themselves on the ground as a shell shrieks and explodes. There is a moment's pause, and gravel and bits of bark tumble about their heads.

"We've got to find that abri. I wish I hadn't lost my flashlight."

"Here it is! No, that stinks too much. Must be the latrine."

"Say, Tom."

"Here."

"Damn, I ran into a tree. I found it."

"All right. Coming."

Martin held out his hand until Randolph bumped into it; then they stumbled together down the rough wooden steps, pulled aside the blanket that served to keep the light in, and found themselves blinking in the low tunnel of the abri.

Brancardiers were asleep in the two tiers of bunks that filled up the sides, and at the table at the end a lieutenant of the medical corps was writing by the light of a smoky lamp.

"They are landing some round here tonight," he said, pointing out two unoccupied bunks. "I'll call you when we need a car."

As he spoke, in succession the three big guns went off. The concussion put the lamp out.

"Damn," said Tom Randolph.

The lieutenant swore and struck a match.

"The red light of the poste de secours is out, too," said Martin.

"No use lighting it again with those unholy mortars . . . It's idiotic to put a poste de secours in the middle of a battery like this."

The Americans lay down to try to sleep. Shell after shell exploded round the dugout, but regularly every few minutes came the hammer blows of the mortars, half the time putting the light out.

A shell explosion seemed to split the dugout

and a piece of éclat whizzed through the blanket that curtained off the door. Someone tried to pick it up as it lay half-buried in the board floor, and pulled his fingers away quickly, blowing on them. The men turned over in the bunks and laughed, and a smile came over the drawn green face of a wounded man who sat very quiet behind the lieutenant, staring at the smoky flame of the lamp.

The curtain was pulled aside and a man staggered in holding with the other hand a limp arm twisted in a mud-covered sleeve, from which blood and mud dripped on to the floor.

"Hello, old chap," said the doctor quietly. A smell of disinfectant stole through the dug-out.

Faint above the incessant throbbing of explosions, the sound of a claxon horn.

"Ha, gas," said the doctor. "Put on your masks, children." A man went along the dugout waking those who were asleep and giving out fresh masks. Someone stood in the doorway blowing a shrill whistle, then there was again the clamour of a claxon near at hand.

The band of the gas mask was tight about Martin's forehead, biting into the skin.

He and Randolph sat side by side on the

edge of the bunk, looking out through the crinkled isinglass eyepieces at the men in the dugout, most of whom had gone to sleep again.

"God, I envy a man who can snore through a gas-mask," said Randolph.

Men's heads had a ghoulish look, strange large eyes and grey oilcloth flaps instead of faces.

Outside the constant explosions had given place to a series of swishing whistles, merging together into a sound as of water falling, only less regular, more sibilant. Occasionally there was the rending burst of a shell, and at intervals came the swingings detonations of the three guns. In the dugout, except for two men who snored loudly, raspingly, everyone was quiet.

Several stretchers with wounded men on them were brought in and laid in the end of the dugout.

Gradually, as the bombardment continued, men began sliding into the dugout, crowding together, touching each other for company, speaking in low voices through their masks.

"A mask, in the name of God, a mask!" a voice shouted, breaking into a squeal, and an unshaven man, with mud caked in his hair and beard, burst through the curtain. His eyelids kept up a continual trembling and the water streamed down both sides of his nose.

"Oh God," he kept talking in a rasping whisper, "Oh God, they're all killed. There were six mules on my waggon and a shell killed them all and threw me into the ditch. You can't find the road any more. They're all killed."

An orderly was wiping his face as if it were a child's.

"They're all killed and I lost my mask. . . . Oh God, this gas. . . ."

The doctor, a short man, looking like a gnome in his mask with its wheezing rubber nosepiece, was walking up and down with short, slow steps.

Suddenly, as three soldiers came in, drawing the curtain aside, he shouted in a shrill, high-pitched voice:

"Keep the curtain closed! Do you want to asphyxiate us?"

He strode up to the newcomers, his voice strident like an angry woman's. "What are you doing here? This is the poste de secours. Are you wounded?"

"But, my lieutenant, we can't stay outside."

"Where's your own cantonment? You can't

stay here; you can't stay here," he shrieked.

"But, my lieutenant, our dugout's been hit."

"You can't stay here. You can't stay here. There's not enough room for the wounded. Name of God!"

"But, my lieutenant . . ."

"Get the hell out of here, d'you hear?"

The men began stumbling out into the darkness, tightening the adjustments of their masks behind their heads.

The guns had stopped firing. There was nothing but the constant swishing and whistling of gas-shells, like endless pails of dirty water being thrown on gravel.

"We've been at it three hours," whispered Martin to Tom Randolph.

"God, suppose these masks need changing."

The sweat from Martin's face steamed in the eyepieces, blinding him.

"Any more masks?" he asked.

A brancardier handed him one. "There aren't any more in the abri."

"I have some more in the car," said Martin.

"I'll get one," cried Randolph, getting to his feet.

They started out of the door together. In the light that streamed out as they drew the flap aside they saw a tree opposite them. A shell exploded, it seemed, right on top of them; the tree rose and bowed towards them and fell.

"Are you all there, Tom?" whispered Martin, his ears ringing.

"Bet your life."

Someone pulled them back into the abri. "Here; we've found another."

Martin lay down on the bunk again, drawing with difficulty each breath. His lips had a wet, decomposed feeling.

At the wrist of the arm he rested his head on, the watch ticked comfortably.

He began to think how ridiculous it would be if he, Martin Howe, should be extinguished like this. The gas-mask might be defective.

God, it would be silly.

Outside the gas-shells were still coming in. The lamp showed through a faint bluish haze. Everyone was still waiting.

Another hour.

Martin began to recite to himself the only thing he could remember, over and over again in time to the ticking of his watch.

> *"Ah, sunflower, weary of time*
> *Ah, sunflower, weary of time*
> *Who countest the steps of the sun;*

Ah, sunflower, weary of time,
Who countest ..."

"One, two, three, four," he counted the shells outside exploding at irregular intervals.

There were periods of absolute silence, when he could hear batteries pong, pong, pong in the distance.

He began again.

"Ah, sunflower, weary of time,
  Who countest the steps of the sun
In search of that far golden clime
  Where the traveller's journey is done.

"Where the youth pined away with desire
  And the pale virgin shrouded in snow
Arise from their graves and aspire
  Where my sunflower wishes to go."

Whang, whang, whang; the battery alongside began again, sending out the light. Someone pulled the blanket aside. A little leprous greyness filtered into the dugout.

"Ah, it's getting light."

The doctor went out and they could hear his steps climbing up to the level of the ground.

Howe saw a man take his mask off and spit.

"Oh, God, a cigarette!" Tom Randolph cried, pulling his mask off.

FIRST ENCOUNTER

The air of the woods was fresh and cool outside. Everything was lost in mist that filled the shellholes as with water and wreathed itself fantastically about the shattered trunks of trees. Here and there was still a little greenish haze of gas. It cut their throats and made their eyes run as they breathed in the cool air of the dawn.

Dawn in a wilderness of jagged stumps and ploughed earth; against the yellow sky, the yellow glare of guns that squat like toads in a tangle of wire and piles of brass shellcases and split wooden boxes. Long rutted roads littered with shellcases stretching through the wrecked woods in the yellow light; strung alongside of them, tangled masses of telephone wires. Torn camouflage fluttering greenish-grey against the ardent yellow sky, and twining among the fantastic black leafless trees, the greenish wraiths of gas. Along the roads camions overturned, dead mules tangled in their traces beside shattered caissons, huddled bodies in long blue coats half buried in the mud of the ditches.

"We've got to pass. . . . We've got five very bad cases."

"Impossible."

"We've got to pass. . . . Sacred name of God!"

"But it is impossible. Two camions are blocked across the road and there are three batteries of seventy-fives waiting to get up the road."

Long lines of men on horseback with gas-masks on, a rearing of frightened horses and jingle of harness.

"Talk to 'em, Howe, for God's sake; we've got to get past."

"I'm doing the best I can, Tom."

"Well, make 'em look lively. Damn this gas!"

"Put your masks on again; you can't breathe without them in this hollow."

"Hay! ye God-damn sons of bitches, get out of the way."

"But they can't."

"Oh, hell, I'll go talk to 'em. You take the wheel."

"No, sit still and don't get excited."

"You're the one's getting excited."

"Damn this gas."

"My lieutenant, I beg you to move the horses to the side of the Road. I have five very badly wounded men. They will die in this gas. I've got to get by."

"God damn him, tell him to hurry."

"Shut up, Tom, for God's sake."

"They're moving. I can't see a thing in this mask."

"Hah, that did for the two back horses."

"Halt! Is there any room in the ambulance? One of my men's just got his thigh ripped up."

"No room, no room."

"He'll have to go to a poste de secours."

The fresh air blowing hard on their faces and the woods getting greener on either side, full of ferns and small plants that half cover the strands of barbed wire and the rows of shells.

At the end of the woods the sun rises golden into a cloudless sky, and on the grassy slope of the valley sheep and a herd of little donkeys are feeding, looking up with quietly moving jaws as the ambulance, smelling of blood and filthy sweat-soaked clothes, rattles by.

Black night. All through the woods along the road squatting mortars spit yellow flame. Constant throbbing of detonations.

Martin, inside the ambulance, is holding together a broken stretcher, while the car jolts slowly along. It is pitch dark in the car, except when the glare of a gun from near the road gives him a momentary view of the man's head, a mass of bandages from the middle of which a little bit of blood-soaked beard sticks out, and of his lean body tossing on the stretcher with every jolt of the car. Martin is kneeling on the floor of the car, his knees bruised by the jolting, holding the man on the stretcher, with his chest pressed on the man's chest and one arm stretched down to keep the limp bandaged leg still.

The man's breath comes with a bubbling sound, now and then mingling with an articulate groan.

"Softly. . . . Oh, softly, oh—oh—oh!"

"Slow as you can, Tom, old man," Martin calls out above the pandemonium of firing on both sides of the road, tightening the muscles of his arm in a desperate effort to keep the limp leg from bouncing. The smell of blood and filth is misery in his nostrils.

"Softly. . . . Softly. . . . Oh — oh — oh!" The groan is barely heard amid the bubbling breath.

Pitch dark in the car. Martin, his every

muscle taut with the agony of the man's pain, is on his knees, pressing his chest on the man's chest, trying with an arm stretched along the man's leg to keep him from bouncing in the broken stretcher.

"Needn't have troubled to have brought him," said the hospital orderly, as blood dripped fast from the stretcher, black in the light of the lantern. "He's pretty near dead now. He won't last long."

CHAPTER VII

"SO you like it, Will? You like this sort of thing?"

Martin Howe was stretched on the grass of a hillside a little above a cross-roads. Beside him squatted a ruddy-faced youth with a smudge of grease on his faintly-hooked nose. A champagne bottle rested against his knees.

"Yes. I've never been happier in my life. It's a coarse boozing sort of a life, but I like it.

They looked over the landscape of greyish rolling hills scarred everywhere by new roads and ranks of wooden shacks. Along the road beneath them crawled like beetles convoy after convoy of motor-trucks. The wind came to them full of a stench of latrines and of the exhaust of motors.

"The last time I saw you," said Martin, after a pause, "was early one morning on the Cambridge bridge. I was walking out from Boston, and we talked of the Eroica they'd played at the Symphony, and you said it was silly to have a great musician try to play soldier. D'you remember?"

"No. That was in another incarnation. Have some fizz."

He poured from the bottle into a battered tin cup.

"But talking about playing soldier, Howe, I must tell you about how our lieutenant got the Croix de Guerre. . . . Somebody ought to write a book called 'Heroisms of the Great War.' . . ."

"I am sure that many people have, and will. You probably'll do it yourself, Will. But go on."

The sun burst from the huddled clouds for a moment, mottling the hills and the scarred valleys with light. The shadow of an aeroplane flying low passed arcoss the field, and the snoring of its motors cut out all other sound.

"Well, our louie's name's Duval, but he spells it with a small 'd' and a big V.' He's been wanting a Croix de Guerre for a hell of a time because lots of fellows in the section have been getting 'em. He tried giving dinners to the General Staff and everything, but that didn't seem to work. So there was nothing to it but to get wounded. So he took to going to the front posts; but the trouble was that it was a hell of a quiet sector and no shells

ever came within a mile of it. At last somebody made a mistake and a little Austrian
eighty-eight came tumbling in and popped
about fifty yards from his staff car. He
showed the most marvellous presence of mind,
'cause he clapped his hand over his eye and
sank back in the seat with a groan. The doctor asked what was the matter, but old Duval
just kept his hand tight over his eye, and said,
'Nothing, nothing; just a scratch,' and went
off to inspect the posts. Of course the posts
didn't need inspecting. And he rode round
all day with a handkerchief over one eye and
a look of heroism in the other. But never
would he let the doctor even peep at it. Next
morning he came out with a bandage round
his head as big as a shiek's turban. He went
to see headquarters in that get-up and
lunched with the staff-officers. Well, he got
his Croix de Guerre all right—cited for as-
suring the evacuation of the wounded under
fire and all the rest of it."

"Some bird. He'll probably get to be a general before the war's over."

Howe poured out the last of the champagne, and threw the bottle listlessly off into
the grass, where it struck an empty shell-case
and broke.

"But, Will, you can't like this," he said. "It's all so like an ash-heap, a huge garbage-dump of men and equipment."

"I suppose it is . . ." said the ruddy-faced youth, discovering the grease on his nose and rubbing it off with the back of his hand. "Damn those dirty Fords. They get grease all over you! I suppose it is that life was so dull in America that anything seems better. I worked a year in an office before leaving home. Give me the garbage-dump."

"Look," said Martin, shading his eyes with his hand and staring straight up into the sky. "There are two planes fighting."

They both screwed up their eyes to stare into the sky, where two bits of mica were circling. Below them, like wads of cotton-wool, some white and others black, were rows of the smoke-puffs of shrapnel from anti-aircraft guns.

The two boys watched the specks in silence. At last one began to grow larger, seemed to be falling in wide spirals. The other had vanished. The falling aeroplane started rising again into the middle sky, then stopped suddenly, burst into flames, and fluttered down behind the hills, leaving an irregular trail of smoke.

"More garbage," said the ruddy-faced youth, as he rose to his feet.

"Shrapnel. What funny place to shoot shrapnel!"

"They must have got the bead on that bunch of material the genie's bringing in."

There was an explosion and a vicious whine of shrapnel bullets among the trees. On the road a staff-car turned round hastily and speeded back.

Martin got up from where he was lying on the grass under a pine tree, looking at the sky, and put his helmet on; as he did so there was another sharp bang overhead and a little reddish-brown cloud that suddenly spread and drifted away among the quiet tree-tops. He took off his helmet and examined it quizzically. "Tom, I've got a dent in the helmet."

Tom Randolph made a grab for the little piece of jagged iron that had rebounded from the helmet and lay at his feet.

"God damn, it's hot," he cried, dropping it; "anyway, finding's keepings." He put his foot on the shrapnel splinter.

"That ought to be mine, I swear, Tom."

"You've got the dent, Howe; what more do you want?"

"Damn hog."

Martin sat on the top step of the dugout, diving down whenever he heard a shell-shriek loudening in the distance. Beside him was a tall man with the crossed cannon of the artillery in his helmet, and a shrunken brown face with crimson-veined cheeks and very long silky black moustaches.

"A dirty business," he said. "It's idiotic. . . . Name of a dog!"

Grabbing each other's arms, they tumbled down the step together as a shell passed overhead to burst in a tree down the road.

"Now look at that." The man held up his musette to Howe. "I've broken the bottle of Bordeaux I had in my musette. It's idiotic."

"Been on permission?"

"Don't I look it?"

They sat at the top of the steps again; the man took out bits of wet glass dripping red wine from his little bag, swearing all the while.

"I was bringing it to the little captain. He's a nice little old chap, the little captain, and he loves good wine."

"Bordeaux?"

"Can't you smell it? It's Medoc, 1900, from my own vines. . . . Look, taste it, there's still a little." He held up the neck of the bottle and Martin took a sip.

The artilleryman drank the rest of it, twisted his long moustaches and heaved a deep sigh.

"Go there, my poor good old wine." He threw the remnants of the bottle into the underbrush. Shrapnel burst a little down the road. "Oh, this is a dirty business! I am a Gascon. . . . I like to live." He put a dirty brown hand on Martin's arm.

"How old do you think I am?"

"Thirty-five"

"I am twenty-four. Look at the picture." From a tattered black note-book held together by an elastic band he pulled a snapshot of a jolly-looking young man with a fleshy face and his hands tucked into the top of a wide, tightly-wound sash. He looked at the picture, smiling and tugging at one of his long moustaches. "Then I was twenty. It's the war." He shrugged his shoulders and put the picture carefully back into his inside pocket. "Oh, it's idiotic!"

"You must have had a tough time."

"It's just that people aren't meant for this sort of thing," said the artilleryman quietly. "You don't get accustomed. The more you see the worse it is. Then you end by going crazy. Oh, it's idiotic!"

"How did you find things at home?"

"Oh, at home! Oh, what do I care about that now? They get on without you. . . . But we used to know how to live, we Gascons. We worked so hard on the vines and on the fruit-trees, and we kept a horse and carriage. I had the best-looking rig in the department. Sunday it was fun; we'd play bowls and I'd ride about with my wife. Oh, she was nice in those days? She was young and fat and laughed all the time. She was something a man could put his arm around, she was. We'd go out in my rig. It was click-clack of the whip in the air and off we were in the broad road. . . . Sacred name of a pig, that one was close. . . . And the Marquis of Montmarieul had a rig, too, but not so good as mine, and my horse would pass his in the road. Oh, it was funny, and he'd look so sour to have common people like us pass him in the road. . . . Boom, there's another. . . . And the Marquis now is nicely embusqué in the automobile service. He is stationed at Versailles. . . . And look at me. . . .

But what do I care about all that now?"

"But after the war . . ."

"After the war?" He spat savagely on the first step of the dugout. "They learn to get on without you."

"But we'll be free to do as we please."

"We'll never forget."

"I shall go to Spain . . ." A piece of shrapnel ripped past Martin's ear, cutting off the sentence.

"Name of God! It's getting hot. . . . Spain: I know Spain." The artilleryman jumped up and began dancing, Spanish fashion, snapping his fingers, his big moustaches swaying and trembling. Several shells burst down the road in quick succession, filling the air with a whine of fragments.

"A cook waggon got it!" the artilleryman shouted, dancing on. "Tra-la la la-la-la-la, la la," he sang, snapping his fingers.

He stopped and spat again.

"What do I care?" he said. "Well, so long, old chap. I must go. . . . Say, let's change knives — a little souvenir."

"Great."

"Good luck."

The artilleryman strode off through the woods, past the portable fence that surrounded the huddled wooden crosses of the graveyard.

Against the red glare of the dawn the wilderness of shattered trees stands out purple, hidden by grey mist in the hollows, looped and draped fantastically with strands of telephone wire and barbed wire, tangled like leafless creepers, that hang in clots against the red sky. Here and there guns squat among piles of shells covered with mottled green cheese-cloth, and spit long tongues of yellow flame agaist the sky. The ambulance waits by the side of the rutted road littered with tin cans and brassshell-cases, while a doctor and two stretcher-bearers bend over a man on a stretcher laid among the underbrush. The man groans and there is a sound of ripping bandages. On the other side of the road a fallen mule feebly wags its head from side to side, a mass of purple froth hanging from its mouth and wide-stretched scarlet nostrils.

There is a new smell in the wind, a smell unutterably sordid, like the smell of the poor immigrants landing at Ellis Island. Martin Howe glances round and sees advancing down the road ranks and ranks of strange grey men whose mushroom-shaped helmets give them an eerie look as of men from the moon in a fairy tale.

"Why, they're Germans," he says to himself; "I'd quite forgotten they existed."

"Ah, they're prisoners." The doctor gets to his feet and glances down the road and then turns to his work again.

The tramp of feet marching in unison on the rough shell-pitted road, and piles and piles of grey men clotted with dried mud, from whom comes the new smell, the sordid, miserable smell of the enemy.

"Things going well?" Martin asks a guard, a man with ashen face and eyes that burn out of black sockets.

"How should I know?"

"Many prisoners?"

"How should I know?"

The captain and the aumonier are taking their breakfast, each sitting on a packing-box with their tin cups and tin plates ranged on the board propped up between them. All round red clay, out of which the abri was excavated. A smell of antiseptics from the door of the dressing-station and of lime and latrines mingling with the greasy smell of the movable kitchen not far away. They are eat-ing dessert, slices of pineapple speared with a knife out of a can. In their manner there is something that makes Martin see vividly two gentlemen in frock-coats dining at a table under the awning of a café on the boulevards. It has a leisurely ceremoniousness, an ease that could exist nowhere else.

"No, my friend," the doctor is saying, "I do not think that an apprehension of religion existed in the mind of palaeolithic man."

"But, my captain, don't you think that you scientific people sometimes lose a little of the significance of things, insisting always on their scientific, in this case on their anthropological, aspect?"

"Not in the least; it is the only way to look at them."

"There are other ways," says the aumonier, smiling.

"One moment. . . ." From under the packing-box the captain produced a small bottle of anisette. "You'll have a little glass, won't you?"

"With the greatest pleasure. What a rarity here, anisette."

"But, as I was about to say, take our life here, for an example." . . . A shell shrieks overhead and crashes hollowly in the woods behind the dugout. Another follows it, exploding nearer. The captain picks a few bits of gravel off the table, reaches for his helmet and continues. "For example, our life here, which is, as was the life of palaeolithic man, taken up only with the bare struggle for existence against overwhelming odds. You know yourself that it is not conducive to religion or any emotion except that of preservation."

"I hardly admit that. . . . Ah, I saved it," the aumonier announces, catching the bottle of anisette as it is about to fall off the table. An exploding shell rends the air about them. There is a pause, and a shower of earth and gravel tumbles about their ears.

"I must go and see if anyone was hurt," says the aumonier, clambering up the clay bank to the level of the ground; "but you will admit, my captain, that the sentiment of preservation is at least akin to the fundamental feelings of religion."

"My dear friend, I admit nothing. . . . Till this evening, good-bye." He waves his hand and goes into the dugout.

Martin and two French soldiers drinking sour wine in the doorway of a deserted house. It was raining outside and now and then a dripping camion passed along the road, slithering through the mud.

"This is the last summer of the war. . . . It must be," said the little man with large brown eyes and a childish, chubby brown face, who sat on Martin's left.

"Why?"

"Oh, I don't know. Everyone feels like that."

"I don't see," said Martin, "why it shouldn't last for ten or twenty years. Wars have before. . . ."

"How long have you been at the front?"

"Six months, off and on."

"After another six months you'll know why it can't go on."

"I don't know; it suits me all right," said the man on the other side of Martin, a man with a jovial red rabbit-like face. "Of course, I don't like being dirty and smelling and all that, but one gets accustomed to it."

"But you are an Alsatian; you don't care."

"I was a baker. They're going to send me to Dijon soon to bake army bread. It'll be a change. There'll be wine and lots of little girls. Good God, how drunk I'll be; and, old chap, you just watch me with the women. . . ."

"I should just like to get home and not be

ordered about," said the first man. "I've been lucky enough, though," he went on; "I've been kept most of the time in reserve. I only had to use my bayonet once."

"When was that?" asked Martin.

"Near Mont Cornélien, last year. We put them to the bayonet and I was running and a man threw his arms up just in front of me saying, "Mon ami, mon ami," in French. I ran on because I couldn't stop, and I heard my bayonet grind as it went through his chest. I tripped over something and fell down."

"You were scared," said the Alsatian.

"Of course I was scared. I was tremblig all over like an old dog in a thunderstorm. When I got up, he was lying on his side with his mouth open and blood running out, my bayonet still sticking into him. You know you have to put your foot against a man and pull hard to get the bayonet out."

"And if you're good at it," cried the Alsatian, "you ought to yank it out as your Boche falls and be ready for the next one. The time they gave me the Croix de Guerre I got three in succession, just like at drill."

"Oh, I was so sorry I had killed him," went on the other Frenchman. "When I went through his pockets I found a post-card. Here it is; I have it." He pulled out a cracked and worn leather wallet, from which he took a photograph and a bunch of pictures. "Look, this photograph was there, too. It hurt my heart. You see, it's a woman and two little girls. They look so nice. . . . It's strange, but I have two children, too, only one's a boy. I lay down on the ground beside him—I was all in—and listened to the machine-guns tapping, put, put, put, put, put, all around. I wished I'd let him kill me instead. That was funny, wasn't it?"

"It's idiotic to feel like that. Put them to the bayonet, all of them, the dirty Boches. Why, the only money I've had since the war began, except my five sous, was fifty francs I found on a German officer. I wonder where he got it, the old corpse-stripper."

"Oh, it's shameful! I am ashamed of being a man. Oh, the shame, the shame . . ." The other man buried his face in his hands.

"I wish they were serving out gniolle for an attack right now," said the Alsatian, "or the gniolle without the attack'd be better yet."

"Wait here," said Martin, "I'll go round to the copé and get a bottle of fizzy. We'll drink to peace or war, as you like. Damn this rain!"

"It's a shame to bury those boots," said the sergeant of the stretcher-bearers.

From the long roll of blanket on the ground beside the hastily-dug grave protruded a pair of high boots, new and well polished as if for parade. All about the earth was scarred with turned clay like raw wounds, and the tilting arms of little wooden crosses huddled together, with here and there a bent wreath or a faded bunch of flowers.

Overhead in the stripped trees a bird was singing.

"Shall we take them off? It's a shame to bury a pair of boots like that."

"So many poor devils need boots."

"Boots cost so dear."

Already two men were lowering the long bundle into the grave.

"Wait a minute; we've got a coffin for him."

A white board coffin was brought.

The boots thumped against the bottom as they put the big bundle in.

An officer strode into the enclosure of the graveyard, flicking his knees with a twig.

"Is this Lieutenant Dupont?" he asked of the sergeant.

"Yes, my lieutenant."

FIRST ENCOUNTER

"Can you see his face?" The officer stooped and pulled apart the blanket where the head was.

"Poor René," he said. "Thank you. Goodbye," and strode out of the graveyard.

The yellowish clay fell in clots on the boards of the coffin. The sergeant bared his head and the aumonier came up, opening his book with a vaguely professional air.

"It was a shame to bury those boots. Boots are so dear nowadays," said the sergeant, mumbling to himself as he walked back towards the little broad shanty they used as a morgue.

Of the house, a little pale salmon-coloured villa only a hell remained, but the garden was quite untouched; fall roses and bunches of white and pink and violet phlox bloomed there among the long grass and the intruding nettles. In the centre the round concrete fountain was no longer full of water, but a few brownish-green toads still inhabited it. The place smelt of box and sweetbriar and yew, and when you lay down on the grass where it grew short under the old yew tree by the fountain, you could see nothing but placid sky and waving green leaves. Martin Howe and

Tom Randolph would spend there the quiet afternoons when they were off duty, sleeping in the languid sunlight, or chatting lazily, pointing out to each other tiny things, the pattern of snail-shells, the glitter of insects' wings, colours, fragrances that made vivid for them suddenly beauty and life, all that the shells that shrieked overhead to explode on the road behind them, threatened to wipe out.

One afternoon Russell joined them, a tall young man with thin face and aquiline nose and unexpectedly light hair.

"Chef says we may go en repos in three days," he said, throwing himself on the ground beside the other two.

"We've heard that before," said Tom Randolph. "Division hasn't started out yet, ole boy; an' we're the last of the division."

"God, I'll be glad to go. . . . I'm dead," said Russell.

"I was up all last night with dysentery."

"So was I. . . . It was not funny; first it'd be vomiting, and then diarrhea, and then the shells'd start coming in. Gave me a merry time of it."

"They say it's the gas," said Martin.

"God, the gas! Turns me sick to think of

it," said Russell, stroking his forehead with his hand. "Did I tell you about what happened to me the night after the attack, up in the woods?"

"No."

"Well, I was bringing a load of wounded down from P. J. Right and I'd got just beyond the corner where the little muddy hill is — you know, where they're always shelling — when I found the road blocked. It was so God-damned black you couldn't see your hand in front of you. A camion'd gone off the road and another had run into it, and everything was littered with boxes of shells spilt about."

"Must have been real nice," said Randolph.

"The devilish part of it was that I was all alone. Coney was too sick with diarrhea to be any use, so I left him up at the post, running out at both ends like he'd die. Well . . . I yelled and shouted like hell in my bad French and blew my whistle and sweated, and the damned wounded inside moaned and groaned. And the shells were coming in so thick I thought my number'd turn up any time. An' I couldn't get anybody. So I just climbed up in the second camion and backed it off into the bushes. . . . God, I bet it'll take a wrecking crew to get it out. . . ."

"That was one good job.

"But there I was with another square in the road and no chance to pass that I could see in that darkness. Then what I was going to tell you about happened. I saw a little bit of light in a ditch beside a big car that seemed to be laying on its side, and I went down to it and there was a bunch of camion drivers, sitting round a lantern drinking.

"'Hello, have a drink!' they called out to me, and one of them got up, waving his arms, ravin' drunk, and threw his arms around me and kissed me on the mouth. His hair and beard were full of wet mud. . . . Then he dragged me into the crowd.

"Ha, here's a copain come to die with us," he cried.

"I gave him a shove and he fell down. But another one got up and handed me a tin cup full of that God-damned gniolle, that I drank not to make 'em sore. Then they all shouted, and stood about me, sayin', 'American's goin' to die with us. He's goin' to drink with us. He's goin' to die with us.' And the shells comin' in all the while. God, I was scared.

"'I want to get a camion moved to the side of the road. . . . Good-bye,' I said. There didn't seem any use talkin' to them.

" 'But you've come to stay with us,' they said, and made me drink some more booze. 'You've come to die with us. Remember you said so.'

"The sweat was running into my eyes so's I could hardly see. I told 'em I'd be right back and slipped away into the dark. Then I thought I'd never get the second camion cranked. At last I managed it and put it so I could squeeze past, but they saw me and jumped up on the running-board of the ambulance, tried to stop the car, all yellin' at once, 'It's no use, the road's blocked both ways. You can't pass. You'd better stay and die with us. Caput.'

"Well, I put my foot on the accelerator and hit one of them so hard with the mud guard he fell into the lantern and put it out. Then I got away. An' how I got past the stuff in that road afterwards was just luck. I couldn't see a God-damn thing; it was so black and I was so nerved up. God, I'll never forget these chap's shoutin', 'Here's a feller come to die with us.' "

"Whew! That's some story," said Randolph.

"That'll make a letter home, won't it?" said

Russell, smiling. "Guess my girl'll think I'm heroic enough after that."

Martin's eyes were watching a big dragon-fly with brown body and cream and rainbow wings that hovered over the empty fountain and the three boys stretched on the grass, and was gone against the azure sky.

The prisoner had grey flesh, so grimed with mud that you could not tell if he were young or old. His uniform hung in a formless clot of mud about a slender frame. They had treated him at the dressing-station for a gash in his upper arm, and he was being used to help the stretcher-bearers. Martin sat in the front seat of the ambulance, watching him listlessly as he walked down the rutted road under the torn shreds of camouflage that fluttered a little in the wind. Martin wondered what he was thinking. Did he accept all this stench and filth and degradation of slavery as part of the divine order of things? Or did he too burn with loathing and revolt?

And all those men beyond the hill and the wood, what were they thinking? But how could they think? The lies they were drunk on would keep them certainly from thinking. They had never had any chance to think until they were hurried into the jaws of it, where there was no room but for laughter and misery and the smell of blood.

The rutted road was empty now. Most of the batteries were quiet. Overhead in the brilliant sky aeroplanes snored monotonously.

The woods all about him were a vast rubbish-heap; the jagged, splintered boles of leafless trees rose in every direction from heaps of brass shell-cases, of tin cans, of bits of uniform and equipment. The wind came in puffs laden with an odour as of dead rats in an attic. And this was what all the centuries of civilisation had struggled for. For this had generations worn away their lives in mines and factories and forges, in fields and workshops, toiling, screwing higher and higher the tension of their minds and muscles, polishing brighter and brighter the mirror of their intelligence. For this!

The German prisoner and another man had appeared in the road again, carrying a stretcher between them, walking with the slow, meticulous steps of great fatigue. A series of shells came in, like three cracks of a whip along the road. Martin followed the stretcher-bearers into the dugout.

The prisoner wiped the sweat from his

grime-streaked forehead, and started up the step of the dugout again, a closed stretcher on his shoulder. Something made Martin look after him as he strolled down the rutted road. He wished he knew German so that he might call after the man and ask him what manner of a man he was.

Again, like snapping of a whip, three shells flashed yellow as they exploded in the brilliant sunlight of the road. The slender figure of the prisoner bent suddenly double, like a pocket-knife closing, and lay still. Martin ran out, stumbling in the hard ruts. In a soft child's voice the prisoner was babbling endlessly, contentendly. Martin kneeled beside him and tried to lift him, clasping him round the chest under the arms. He was very hard to lift, for his legs dragged limply in their soaked trousers, where the blood was beginning to saturate the muddy, cloth, stickily. Sweat dripped from Martin's face on the man's face, and he felt the arm-muscles and the ribs pressed against his body as he clutched the wounded man tightly to him in the effort of carrying him towards the dugout. The effort gave Martin a strange contentment. It was as if his body were taking part in the agony of this man's body. At last they were washed out, all the hatreds, all the lies, in blood and sweat. Nothing was left but the quiet friendliness of beings alike in every part, eternally alike.

Two men with a stretcher came from the dugout, and Martin laid the man's body, fast growing limper, less animated, down very carefully.

As he stood by the car, wiping the blood off his hands with an oily rag, he could still feel the man's ribs and the muscles of the man's arm against his side. It made him strangely happy.

At the end of the dugout a man was drawing short, hard breaths as if he'd been running. There was the accustomed smell of blood and chloride and bandages and filthy miserable flesh. Howe lay on a stretcher wrapped in his blanket, with his coat over him, trying to sleep. There was very little light from a smoky lamp down at the end where the wounded were. The French batteries were fairly quiet, but the German shells were combing through the woods, coming in series of three and four, gradually nearing the dugout and edging away again. Howe saw the woods as a gambling table on which,

throw after throw, scattered the random dice
of death.

He pulled his blanket up round his head.
He must sleep. How silly to think about it.
It was luck. If a shell had his number on it
he'd be gone before the words were out of his
mouth. How silly that he might be dead any
minute! What right had a nasty little piece
of tinware to go tearing through his rich,
feeling flesh, extinguishing it?

Like the sound of a mosquito in his ear,
only louder, more vicious, a shell-shriek
shrilled to the crash.

Damn! How foolish, how supremely silly
that tired men somewhere away in the woods
the other side of the lines should be shoving
a shell into the breach of a gun to kill him,
Martin Howe!

Like dice thrown on a table, shells burst
about the dugout, now one side, now the
other.

"Seem to have taken a fancy to us this
evening'," Howe heard Tom Randolph's voice
from the bunk opposite.

"One," muttered Martin to himself, as he
lay frozen with fear, flat on his back, biting
his trembling lips, "two. . . .God, that was
near!"

A dragging instant of suspense, and the shriek growing loud out of the distance.

"This is us." He clutched the sides of the stretcher.

A snorting roar rocked the dugout. Dirt fell in his face. He looked about, dazed. The lamp was still burning. One of the wounded men, with a bandage like an Arab's turban about his head, sat up in his stretcher with wide, terrified eyes.

"God watches over drunkards and the feeble-minded. Don't let's worry, Howe," shouted Randolph from his bunk.

"That probably bitched car No 4 for evermore," he answered, turning on his stretcher, relieved for some reason from the icy suspense.

"We should worry! We'll foot it home, that's all."

The casting of the dice began again, farther away this time.

"We won that throw," thought Martin.

CHAPTER VIII

DUCKS quacking woke Martin. For a
moment he could not think where he
was; then he remembered. The rafters of
the loft of the farmhouse over his head were
hung with bunches of herbs drying. He lay
a long while on his back looking at them,
sniffing the sweetened air, while farmyard
sounds occupied his ears, hens cackling, the
grunting of pigs, the rou-cou-cou-cou, rou-
cou-cou-cou of pigeons under the eaves. He
stretched himself and looked about him. He
was alone except for Tom Randolph, who
slept in a pile of blankets next to the wall,
his head, with its close-cropped black hair,
pillowed on his bare arm. Martin slipped
off the canvas cot he had slept on and went
to the window of the loft, a little square open
at the level of the floor, through which came
a dazzle of blue and gold and green. He
looked out. Stables and hay-barns filled two
sides of the farmyard below him. Behind
them was a mass of rustling oak-trees. On
the lichen-greened tile roofs pigeons strutted
about, putting their coral feet daintily one

before the other, puffing out their glittering breasts. He breathed deep of the smell of hay and manure and cows and of unpolluted farms.

From the yard came a riotous cackling of chickens and quacking of ducks, mingled with the peeping of the little broods. In the middle a girl in blue gingham, sleeves rolled up as far as possible on her brown arms, a girl with a mass of dark hair loosely coiled above the nape of her neck, was throwing to the fowls handfuls of grain with a wide gesture.

"And to think that only yesterday . . ." said Martin to himself. He listened carefully for some time. "Wonderful! You can't even hear the guns."

CHAPTER IX

THE evening was pearl-grey when they left the village; in their nostrils was the smell of the leisurely death of the year, of leaves drying and falling, of ripened fruit and bursting seed-pods.

"The fall's a maddening sort o' time for me." said Tom Randolph. "It makes me itch to get up on ma hind legs an' do things, go places."

"I suppose it's that the earth has such a feel of accomplishment," said Howe.

"You do feel as if Nature had pulled off her part of the job and was restin'."

They stopped a second and looked about them, breathing deep. On one side of the road were woods where in long alleys the mists deepened into purple darkness.

'There's the moon."

"God! it looks like a pumpkin."

"I wish those guns'd shut up 'way off there to the north."

"They're sort of irrelevant, aren't they?"

They walked on, silent, listening to the guns

throbbing far away, like muffled drums beaten in nervous haste.

"Sounds almost like a barrage."

Martin for some reason was thinking of the last verses of Shelley's Hellas. He wished he knew them so that he could recite them:

"Faiths and empires gleam
Like wrecks in a dissolving dream."

The purple trunks of saplings passed slowly across the broad face of the moon as they walked along. How beautiful the world was!

"Look, Tom." Martin put his arm about Randolph's shoulder and nodded towards the moon. "It might be a ship with puffed-out pumpkin-coloured sails, the way the trees make it look now."

"Wouldn't it be great to go to sea?" said Randolph, looking straight into the moon, "an' get out of this slaughter-house. It's nice to see the war, but I have no intention of taking up butchery as a profession. . . . There is too much else to do in the world."

They walked slowly along the road talking of the sea, and Martin told how when he was a little kid he'd had an uncle who used to tell him about the Vikings and the Swan Path, and how one of the great moments of his life had been when he and a friend had looked out

of their window in a little inn on Cape Cod
one morning and seen the sea and the swaying
gold path of the sun on it, stretching away,
beyond the horizon.

"Poor old life," he said. "I'd expected to
do so much with you." And they both
laughed, a little bitterly.

They were strolling past a large farmhouse
that stood like a hen among chicks in a crowd
of little outbuildings. A man in the road lit a
cigarette and Martin recognised him in the
orange glare of the match.

"Monsieur Merrier!" He held out his hand.
It was the aspirant he had drunk beer with
weeks ago at Brocourt.

"Hah! It's you!"

"So you are en repos here, too?"

"Yes, indeed. But you two come in and
see us; we are dying of the blues."

"We'd love to stop in for a second."

A fire smouldered in the big hearth of the
farmhouse kitchen, sending a little irregular
fringe of red light out over the tiled floor.
At the end of the room towards the door three
men were seated round a table, smoking. A
candle threw their huge and grotesque shadows on the floor and on the whitewashed
walls, and lit up the dark beams of that part

of the ceiling. The three men got up and everyone shook hands, filling the room with swaying giant shadows. Champagne was brought and tin cups and more candles, and the Americans were given the two most comfortable chairs.

"Its such a find to have Americans who speak French," said a bearded man with unusually large brilliant eyes. He had been introduced as André Dubois, "a very terrible person," had added Merrier, laughing. The cork popped out of the bottle he had been struggling with.

"You see, we never can find out what you think about things. . . . All we can do is to be sympathetically inane, and 'vive les braves alliés' and that sort of stuff."

"I doubt if we Americans do think," said Martin.

"Cigarettes, who wants some cigarettes?" cried Lully, a small man with a very brown oval face to which long eyelashes and a little bit of silky black moustache gave almost a winsomeness. When he laughed he showed brilliant, very regular teeth. As he handed the cigarettes about he looked searchingly at Martin with eyes disconcertingly intense. "Merrier has told us about you," he said.

"You seem to be the first American we've met who agreed with us."

"What about?"

"About the war, of course."

"Yes," took up the fourth man, a blonde Norman with an impressive, rather majestic face, "we were very interested. You see, we bore each other, talking always among ourselves. . . . I hope you won't be offended if I agree with you in saying that Americans never think. I've been in Texas, you see."

"Really?"

"Yes, I went to a Jesuit College in Dallas. I was preparing to enter the Society of Jesus."

"How long have you been in the war?" asked André Dubois, passing his hand across his beard.

"We've both been in the same length of time — about six months."

"Do you like it?"

"I don't have a bad time. . . . But the people in Boccaccio managed to enjoy themselves while the plague was at Florence. That seems to me the only way to take the war."

"We have no villa to take refuge in, though," said Dubois, "and we have forgotten all our amusing stories."

"And in America—they like the war?"

"They don't know what it is. They are like children. They believe everything they are told, you see; they have had no experience in international affairs, like you Europeans. To me our entrance into the war is a tragedy."

"It's sort of goin' back on our only excuse for existin,'" put in Randolph.

"In exchange for all the quiet and the civilisation and the beauty of ordered lives that Europeans gave up in going to the new world we gave them opportunity to earn luxury, and, infinitely more important, freedom from the past, that gangrened ghost of the past that is killing Europe to-day with its infection of hate and greed of murder."

"America has turned traitor to all that, you see; that's the way we look at it. Now we're a military nation, an organized pirate like France and England and Germany."

"But American idealism? The speeches, the notes?" cried Lully, catching the edge of the table with his two brown hands.

"Camouflage," said Martin.

"You mean it's insincere?"

"The best camouflage is always sincere."

Dubois ran his hands through his hair.

"Of course, why should there be any difference?" he said.

"Oh, we're all dupes, we're all dupes. Look, Lully, old man, fill up the Americans' glasses."

"Thanks."

"And I used to believe in liberty," said Martin. He raised his tumbler and looked at the candle through the pale yellow champagne. On the wall behind him, his arm and hand and the tumbler were shadowed huge in dusky lavender blue. He noticed that his was the only tumbler.

"I am honoured," he said; "mine is the only glass."

"And that's looted," said Merrier.

"It's funny . . ." Martin suddenly felt himself filled with a desire to talk. "All my life I've struggled for my own liberty in my small way. Now I hardly know if the thing exists."

"Exists? Of course it does, or people wouldn't hate it so," cried Lully.

"I used to think," went on Martin, "that it was my family I must escape from to be free; I mean all the conventional ties, the worship of success and the respectabilities that is drummed into you when you're young."

"I suppose everyone has thought that. . . ."

"How stupid we were before the war, how we prated of small revolts, how we sniggered over little jokes at religion and government. And all the while, in the infinite greed, in the infinite stupidity of men, this was being prepared." André Dubois was speaking, puffing nervously at a cigarette between phrases, now and then pulling at his beard with a long, sinewy hand.

"What terrifies me rather is their power to enslave our minds," Martin went on, his voice growing louder and surer as his idea carried him along. "I shall never forget the flags, the menacing exultant flags along all the streets before we went to war, the gradual unbarring of teeth, gradual lulling to sleep of people's humanity and sense by the phrases, the phrases. . . . America, as you know, is ruled by the press. And the press is ruled by whom? Who shall ever know what dark forces bought and bought until we should be ready to go blinded and gagged to war?. . . People seem to so love to be fooled. Intellect used to mean freedom, a light struggling against darkness. Now the darkness is using the light for its own purposes. . . . We are slaves of bought intellect, willing slaves."

"But, Howe, the minute you see that and laugh at it, you're not a slave. Laugh and be individually as decent as you can, and don't worry your head about the rest of the world; and have a good time in spite of the God-damned scoundrels," broke out Randolph in English. "No use worryin' yourself into the grave over a thing you can't help."

"There is one solution and one only, my friends," said the blonde Norman; "the Church. . . ." He sat up straight in his chair, speaking slowly with expressionless face. "People are too weak and too kindly to shift for themselves. Government of some sort there must be. Lay Government has proved through all the tragic years of history to be merely a ruse of the strong to oppress the weak, of the wicked to fool the confiding. There remains only religion. In the organisation of religion lies the natural and suitable arrangement for the happiness of man. The Church will govern not through physical force but through spiritual force."

"The force of fear." Lully jumped to his feet impatiently, making the bottles sway on the table.

"The force of love. . . . I once thought as you do, my friend," said the Norman, pulling

Lully back into his chair with a smile.

Lully drank a glass of champagne greedily and undid the buttons of his blue jacket.

"Go on," he said; "it's madness."

"All the evil of the Church," went on the Norman's even voice, "comes from her struggles to attain supremacy. Once assured of triumph, established as the rule of the world, it becomes the natural channel through which the wise rule and direct the stupid, not for their own interest, not for ambition for wordly things, but for the love that is in them, the freedom. It denies the world, and the slaveries and rewards of it. It gives the love of God as the only aim of life."

"But think of the Church to-day, the cardinals at Rome, the Church turned everywhere to the worship of tribal gods. . . ."

"Yes, but admit that that can be changed. The Church has been supreme in the past; can it not again be supreme? All the evil comes from the struggle, from the compromise. Picture to yourself for a moment a world conquered by the Church, ruled through the soul and mind, where force will not exist, where instead of all the multitudinous tyrannies man has choked his life with in organising against other men, will exist the one supreme thing, the Church of God. Instead of many hatreds, one love. Instead of many slaveries, one freedom."

"A single tyranny, instead of a million. What's the choice?" cried Lully.

"But you are both violent, my children." Merrier got to his feet and smilingly filled the glasses all around. "You go at the matter too much from the heroic point of view. All this sermonising does no good. We are very simple people who want to live quietly and have plenty to eat and have no one worry us or hurt us in the little span of sunlight before we die. All we have now is the same war between the classes; those that exploit and those that are exploited. The cunning, unscrupulous people control the humane, kindly people. This war that has smashed our little European world in which order was so painfully taking the place of chaos, seems to me merely a gigantic battle fought over the plunder of the world by the pirates who have grown fat to the point of madness on the work of their own people, on the work of the millions in Africa, in India, in America, who have come directly or indirectly under the yoke of the insane greed of the white races. Well, our edifice is ruined. Let's think no more of it.

Ours is now the duty of rebuilding, reorganising. I have not faith enough in human nature to be an anarchist. . . . We are too like sheep; we must go in flocks, and a flock to live must organise. There is plenty for everyone, even with the huge growth in population all over the world. What we want is organisation from the bottom, organisation by the ungreedy, by the humane, by the uncunning, socialism of the masses that shall spring from the natural need of men to help one another; not socialism from the top to the ends of the governors, that they may clamp us tighter in their fetters. We must stop the economic war, the war for existence of man against man. That will be the first step in the long climb to civilisation. They must co-operate, they must learn that it is saner and more advantageous to help one another than to hinder one another in the great war against nature. And the tyranny of the feudal money lords, the unspeakable misery of this war is driving men closer together into fraternity, co-operation. It is the lower classes, therefore, that the new world must be founded on. The rich must be extinguished; with them wars will die. First between rich and poor, between the exploiter and the exploited. . . ."

"They have one thing in common," interrupted the blonde Norman, smiling.

"What's that?"

"Humanity. . . . That is, feebleness, cowardice."

"No, indeed. All through the world's history there has been one law for the lord and another for the slave, one humanity for the lord and another humanity for the slave. What we must strive for is a true universal humanity."

"True," cried Lully, "but why take the longest, the most difficult road? You say that people are sheep; they must be driven. I say that you and I and our American friends here are not sheep. We are capable of standing alone, of judging all for ourselves, and we are just ordinary people like anyone else."

"Oh, but look at us, Lully!" interrupted Merrier. "We are too weak and too cowardly. . . ."

"An example," said Martin, excitedly leaning across the table. "We none of us believe that war is right or useful or anything but a hideous method of mutual suicide. Have we the courage of our own faith?"

"As I said," Merrier took up again, "I have too little faith to be an anarchist, but I have too much to believe in religion." His tin cup rapped sharply on the table as he set it down.

"No," Lully continued, after a pause, "it is better for man to worship God, his image on the clouds, the creation of his fancy, than to worship the vulgar apparatus of organised life, government. Better sacrifice his children to Moloch than to that society for the propagation and protection of commerce, the nation. Oh, think of the cost of government in all the ages since men stopped living in marauding tribes! Think of the great men martyred. Think of the thought trodden into the dust. . . . Give man a chance for once. Government should be purely utilitarian, like the electric light wires in a house. It is a method for attaining peace and comfort—a bad one, I think, at that; not a thing to be worshipped as God. The one reason for it is the protection of property. Why should we have property? That is the central evil of the world. . . . That is the cancer that has made life a hell of misery until now; the inflated greed of it has spurred on our nations of the West to throw themselves back, for ever, perhaps, into the depths of savagery. . . . Oh, if people would only trust their own fundamental kindliness, the fraternity, the love that is the strongest thing in life. Abolish property, and the disease of the desire for it, the desire to grasp and have, and you'll need no government to protect you. The vividness and resiliency of the life of man is being fast crushed under organisation, tabulation. Over-organisation is death. It is disorganisation, not organisation, that is the aim of life."

"I grant that what all of you say is true, but why say it over and over again?" André Dubois talked, striding back and forth beside the table, his arms gesticulating. His compound shadow thrown by the candles on the white wall followed him back and forth, mocking him with huge blurred gestures. "The Greek philosophers said it and the Indian sages. Our descendants thousands of years from now will say it and wring their hands as we do. Has not someone on earth the courage to act? . . ." The men at the table turned towards him, watching his tall figure move back and forth.

"We are slaves. We are blind. We are deaf. Why should we argue, we who have no experience of different things to go on? It has always been the same: man the slave of property or religion, of his own shadow. . . . First we must burst our bonds, open our eyes, clear our ears. No we know nothing but what we are told by the rulers. Oh, the lies, the lies, the lies, the lies that life is smothered in! We must strike once more for freedom, for the sake of the dignity of man. Hopelessly, cynically, ruthlessly we must rise and show at least that we are not taken in; that we are slaves but not willing slaves. Oh, they have deceived us so many times. We have been such dupes, we have been such dupes!"

"You are right," said the blonde Norman sullenly; "we have all been dupes."

A sudden self-consciousness chilled them all to silence for a while. Without wanting to, they strained their ears to hear the guns. There they were, throbbing loud, unceasing, towards the north, like hasty muffled drumbeating.

> *Cease; drain not to its dregs the wine,*
> *Of bitter Prophecy.*
> *The world is weary of its past.*
> *Oh, might it die or rest at last.*

All through the talk snatches from "Hellas" had been running through Howe's head.

After a long pause he turned to Merrier and asked him how he had fared in the attack.

"Oh, not so badly. I brought my skin

back," said Merrier, laughing. "It was a dull business. After waiting eight hours under gas bombardment we got orders to advance, and so over we went with the barrage way ahead of us. There was no resistance where we were. We took a lot of prisoners and blew up some dugouts and I had the good luck to find a lot of German chocolate. It came in handy, I can tell you, as no ravitaillement came for two days. We just had biscuits and I toasted the biscuits and chocolate together and had quite good meals, though I nearly died of thirst afterwards. . . . We lost heavily, though, when they started counterattacking."

"An' no one of you were touched?"

"Luck. . . . But we lost many dear friends. Oh, it's always like that."

"Look what I brought back — a German gun," said André Dubois, going to the corner of the room.

"That's some souvenir," said Tom Randolph, sitting up suddenly, shaking himself out of the reverie he had been sunk in all through the talk of the evening.

"And I have three hundred rounds. They'll come in handy some day."

"When?"

"In the revolution—after the war."

"That's the stuff I like to hear," cried Randolph, getting to his feet. "Why wait for the war to end?"

"Why? Because we have not the courage. . . . But it is impossible until after the war."

"And then you think it is possible?"

"Yes."

"Will it accomplish anything?"

"God knows."

"One last bottle of champagne," cried Merrier.

They seated themselves round the table again. Martin took in at a glance the eager sunburned faces, the eyes burning with hope, with determination, and sudden joy flared through him.

"Oh, there is hope," he said, drinking down his glass. "We are too young, too needed to fail. We must find a way, find the first step of a way to freedom, or life is a hollow mockery."

"To Revolution, to Anarchy, to the Socialist state," they all cried, drinking down the last of the champagne. All the candles but one had guttered out. Their shadows swayed and darted in long arms and changing, grotesque limbs about the room.

"But first there must be peace," said the Norman, Jean Chenier, twisting his mouth into a faintly bitter smile.

"Oh, indeed, there must be peace."

"Of all slaveries, the slavery of war, of armies, is the bitterest, the most hopeless slavery." Lully was speaking, his smooth brown face in a grimace of excitement and loathing. "War is our first enemy."

"But oh, my friend," said Merrier, "we will win in the end. All the people in all the armies of the world believe as we do. In all the minds the seed is sprouting."

"Before long the day will come. The tocsin will ring."

"Do you really believe that?" cried Martin. "Have we the courage, have we the energy, have we the power? Are we the men our ancestors were?"

"No," said Dubois, crashing down on the table with his fist; "we are merely intellectuals. We cling to a mummified world. But they have the power and the nerve."

"Who?"

"The stupid average working-people."

"We only can combat the lies," said Lully; "they are so easily duped. After the war that is what we must do."

"Oh, but we are all such dupes," cried Dubois. "First we must fight the lies. It is the lies that choke us."

It was very late. Howe and Tom Randolph were walking home under a cold white moon already well sunk in the west; northward was a little flickering glare above the tops of the low hills and a sound of firing as of muffled drums beaten hastily.

"With people like that we needn't despair of civilisation," said Howe.

"With people who are young and aren't scared you can do lots."

"We must come over and see those fellows again. It's such a relief to be able to talk."

"And they give you the idea that something's really going on in the world, don't they?"

"Oh, it's wonderful! Think that the awakening may come soon."

"We might wake up to-morrow and . . ."

"It's too important to joke about; don't be an ass, Tom."

They rolled up in their blankets in the silent barn and listened to the drum-fire in the distance. Martin saw again, as he lay on his side with his eyes closed, the group of men in blue uniforms, men with eager brown faces and eyes gleaming with hope, and saw their full red lips moving as they talked.

The candle threw the shadows of their heads, huge, fantastic, and of their gesticulating arms on the white walls of the kitchen. And it seemed to Martin Howe that all his friends were gathered in that room.

CHAPTER X

"THEY say you sell shoe-laces," said Martin, his eyes blinking in the faint candlelight.

Crouched in the end of the dugout was a man with a brown skin like wrinkled leather, and white eyebrows and moustaches. All about him were piles of old boots, rotten with wear and mud, holding fantastically the imprints of the toes and ankle-bones of the feet that had worn them. The candle cast flitting shadows over them so that they seemed to move back and forth faintly, as do the feet of wounded men laid out on the floor of the dressing-station.

"I'm a cobbler by profession," said the man. He made a gesture with the blade of his knife in the direction of a huge bundle of leather laces that hung from a beam above his head. "I've done all those since yesterday. I cut up old boots into laces."

"Helps out the five sous a bit." said Martin, laughing.

"This post is convenient for my trade," went on the cobbler as he picked out another boot to be cut into laces, and started hacking the upper part off the worn sole. "At the little hut, where they pile up the stiffs before they bury them—you know, just to the left outside the abri—they leave lots of their boots around. I can pick up any number I want." With a clasp-knife he was cutting the leather in a spiral, paring off a thin lace. He contracted his bushy eyebrows as he bent over his work. The candlelight glinted on the knife blade as he twisted it about dexterously.

"Yes, many a good copain of mine has had his poor feet in those boots. What of it? Some day another fellow will be making laces out of mine, eh?" He gave a wheezy, coughing laugh.

"I guess I'll take a pair. How much are they?"

"Six sous."

"Good."

The coins glinted in the light of the candle as they clinked in the man's leather-blackened palm.

"Good-bye," said Martin. He walked past men sleeping in the bunks on either side as he went towards the steps.

At the end of the dugout the man crouched on his pile of the leather, with his knife that glinted in the candlelight dexterously carving laces out of the boots of those who no longer need them.

CHAPTER XI

THERE is no sound in the poste de secours. A faint greenish light filters down from the quiet woods outside. Martin is kneeling beside a stretcher where lies a mass of torn blue uniform crossed in several places by strips of white bandages clotted with dark blood. The massive face, grimed with mud, is very waxy and grey. The light hair hangs in clots about the forehead. The nose is sharp, but there is a faint smile about the lips made thin by pain.

"Is there anything I can get you?" asks Martin softly.

"Nothing." Slowly the blue eyelids uncover hazel eyes that burn feverishly.

"But you haven't told me yet, how's Merrier?"

"A shell . . . dead . . . poor chap."

"And the anarchist, Lully?"

"Dead."

"And Dubois?"

"Why ask?" came the faint rustling voice peevishly. "Everybody's dead. You're dead, aren't you?"

"No, I'm alive, and you. A little courage. . . . We must be cheerful."

"It's not for long. To-morrow, the next day. . . ." The blue eyelids slip back over the crazy burning eyes and the face takes on again the waxen look of death.

THE END

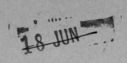